★ # Harry S. Truman

Missouri Farm Boy

Illustrated by Robert Doremus

Harry S. Truman

Missouri Farm Boy

by Wilma J. Hudson

Aladdin Books
Macmillan Publishing Company   New York
Maxwell Macmillan Canada   Toronto
Maxwell Macmillan International
New York   Oxford   Singapore   Sydney

First Aladdin Books edition 1992
Aladdin Books   Maxwell Macmillan Canada, Inc.
Macmillan Publishing Company   1200 Eglinton Avenue East
866 Third Avenue   Suite 200
New York, NY 10022   Don Mills, Ontario M3C 3N1

Macmillan Publishing Company is part of the Maxwell Communication
Group of Companies.

Printed in the United States of America
10   9   8   7   6   5   4   3   2   1

Library of Congress Cataloging-in-Publication Data
Hudson, Wilma J.
    Harry S. Truman : Missouri farm boy / by Wilma J. Hudson;
[illustrated by Robert Doremus] — 1st Aladdin Books ed.
        p.   cm. — (Childhood of Famous Americans)
    Originally published: Indianapolis : Bobbs-Merrill, 1973.
    Summary: A biography stressing the childhood of the Missouri farm
boy who became the thirty-third president.
    ISBN 0-689-71658-3
    1. Truman, Harry S., 1884–1972—Childhood and youth—Juvenile
literature.   2. Presidents—United States—Biography—Juvenile
literature.   [1. Truman, Harry S., 1884–1972—Childhood and
youth.   2. Presidents.]   I. Doremus, Robert, ill.   II. Title.
III. Series: Childhood of Famous Americans series.
[E814.H82   1992]
973.918′092—dc20
[B]   92-7513

To Mother and Dad

Acknowledgements:
The author wishes to express her gratitude to Mr. Harry S. Truman and his secretary, Miss Rose A. Conway, for their gracious assistance. She wishes also to thank the following for their help in her research at the Harry S. Truman Library: Mr. Philip C. Brooks, Director; Mr. Philip D. Lagerquist, Research Archivist; and the staff of Photography Files. Sources of factual information included Memoirs. Volume I: Years of Decision and Volume II: Years of Trial and Hope and Mr. Citizen by Harry S. Truman.

Illustrations

Full pages

Numerous smaller illustrations

Contents

★ # Harry S. Truman

Missouri Farm Boy

A Little Boy
on a Big Farm

"DON'T YOU WANT to lie down with Vivian to take an afternoon nap?" asked Martha Truman.

"No, Mama," replied Harry. "I'm not sleepy. Let me look at pictures."

Young Harry S. Truman, holding the big family Bible, sat in a big chair in the dining room. His brother Vivian, two years younger, lay sound asleep nearby on the floor. Their black and tan dog, Tandy, was stretched out beside Vivian. Another pet, a Maltese kitten, slept on the hearth in front of the fireplace.

Harry's mother went back to her work in the kitchen, but moments later bedlam broke loose in the dining room. Suddenly the Maltese kitten jumped up from the hearth, mewed pitifully, and raced wildly to a corner of the room. The black and tan dog jumped up and started to bark loudly. Little Vivian, awakened and frightened by the noise, started to cry. "Mama, come quick," called Harry, also frightened.

Martha Truman rushed back into the dining room and took a quick glance. At once she could tell that something had happened to the kitten. "Kitty is hurt," she cried. "Maybe he has been burned by a spark from the fireplace."

"Oh no!" exclaimed Harry. "Poor Kitty. I just don't want Kitty to be hurt."

Quickly Harry's mother picked up Vivian from the floor and ordered Tandy to stop barking. Then she led Harry to the corner of the room where the kitten still was wailing loudly. "Here, Kitty," she said tenderly. "Have you been burned by a spark from the fireplace?"

In a minute or so Grandpa Young burst into the room. "What is causing all this noise?" he cried. "I heard it way out in the yard."

Harry rushed over to meet his grandfather. "Kitty is hurt," he replied.

"Yes," explained Harry's mother. "He was sleeping on the hearth in front of the fireplace. Maybe a spark popped out and burned him. You can tell that he is hurt by the way he is crying."

Grandpa Young walked over and picked up the wailing kitten. "Well, no wonder he is crying so loudly," he exclaimed. "The end of his tail is almost burned off. We must put something on it at once."

"What do you need?" asked Harry's mother.

"Bring me a rag, a string, and a spoonful of butter," said Grandpa Young. "Then I'll put a bandage on his tail."

Harry's mother quickly brought the rag,

string, and butter. She helped to hold the kitten while Grandpa Young treated and bandaged his tail. Harry stood by and watched. "Now will his tail get well?" he asked.

"No," replied Grandpa Young, "but the bandage and butter will keep his tail from hurting so much. It is badly burned and I'm afraid we'll have a bobtailed cat around here."

During the following days Harry and Vivian took good care of the injured kitten. Harry began to call him Bobtail. "Here, Bobtail," he said. "Come, drink your milk."

Vivian tried to call the kitten Bobtail, too, but left off the end because he found the word a little too much to say. "Here, Bob," he said. "Come, drink your milk."

Soon both the boys began to call the injured kitten Bob, which Vivian could say without trouble. Already they had named their dog Tandy because he was partly tan in color.

The Truman family included John Truman, his wife, Martha, and their two sons, Harry and Vivian. They now lived with Martha's parents, Solomon and Harriet Young, on a big farm of six hundred acres. This farm was located six miles from Belton in western Missouri, about eighteen miles south of Kansas City. John Truman managed the farm and Martha helped with the housework. Harry, now past four years old, liked living on the big farm.

John and Martha Truman had started housekeeping in the village of Lamar in Barton County, Missouri, where Harry had been born, May 8, 1884. About a year later they had moved northward to a farm in Cass County, where Vivian, two years younger than Harry, had been born. Then soon after Vivian's birth, they had moved in with Martha's parents still farther north in Jackson County, where they now lived.

One afternoon in early summer while Vivian was taking a nap on the dining room floor, Harry wandered around the yard with Tandy and Bob. He strolled here and there, wishing he could find something more to do. Finally he walked out to the orchard and climbed into an apple tree.

As he sat in the tree, he looked out across the big fields on the farm. He had never been far from the house and wondered what there might be out there to see. Soon he decided to find out. He climbed down carefully to the ground and started to walk along a path with his two faithful pets running along beside him.

Back at the house Grandpa Young was picking wild strawberries and carrying them to the kitchen. Inside the kitchen Grandma Young and Martha Truman were busy cleaning and cooking the strawberries. They used them for making a strawberry shortcake and jam.

Once, as Grandma Young was filling a jar with fresh strawberry jam, she said, "Harry and Vivian surely will enjoy this jam next winter."

"Yes, they both like bread loaded with jam," replied Martha. "The jam will be especially good for them to eat between meals."

Just then Vivian awoke from his nap and appeared at the door. "I'm hungry," he said.

Martha smiled. "I guess we can begin to use some of that jam right now," she said to her mother. Then, turning to Vivian, she asked, "How would you like a slice of bread spread with fresh strawberry jam?"

"Oh good!" cried Vivian.

Martha prepared the bread and jam and placed Vivian on a chair at the kitchen table. After he finished eating, she said, "Now run outdoors to play with Harry. He's out there somewhere with Tandy and Bob. We've been so busy I haven't looked for him lately."

Vivian went outdoors and started to look all about the yard for Harry but couldn't find him. He tried to locate him by calling, but there was no answer. Before long he hurried back into the house and cried, "Mama, no Harry." His speech was too limited to explain.

"Where do you suppose he can be?" said Martha, still not alarmed. She went outside and walked around the house calling, "Harry! Answer me! Where in the world are you?" Once more there was no answer.

By now Mama was becoming alarmed. She rushed back into the house and told Grandma Young, "We can't find Harry. He may have crawled off somewhere and gone to sleep. You look around for him in the rooms downstairs and I will look for him upstairs."

Just as they returned from searching, Cousin Sol Chiles, a teenage relative who worked part-time on the farm, came to the house. "Oh

Sol," cried Martha, "come help us to find Harry. We have been so busy working that we have neglected to watch him. When we last saw him, he was playing outside in the yard with Tandy and Bob. Now he's gone, and we can't find him."

"Well, this afternoon while I was working near the barn, I saw him sitting in an apple tree," said Cousin Sol. "Then he climbed down and took off down a path with Tandy and Bob. Probably they're still out there on the farm."

In the midst of this conversation, Grandpa Young came to the house. He was greatly alarmed when he found that Harry was missing. "We must organize a search party at once to find him," he said. "Martha, you stay here at the house and watch for him while Grandma, Cousin Sol, and I look for him out on the farm."

The three walked out the back door and paused a moment to talk. "We'll have to split up in order to look thoroughly," said Grandpa Young. "There are three lanes that lead to different parts of the farm. Sol, you take the left lane, Grandma, you take the center lane, and I'll take the right lane."

Each searcher started off down a lane, calling for Harry and looking for signs that he may have been there. Grandpa followed a lane that led through a pasture where many cattle were grazing. All the while he kept calling, "Harry! Harry!" but all he could hear were Grandma and Cousin Sol calling for Harry, too.

Before long Grandpa Young came to a big field of corn with growing cornstalks and leaves hiding the ground in all directions. He opened the gate, stepped inside, and gazed hopelessly out over the field. "Now I don't know which way to go," he said. "It's almost impossible to look for anybody here in this corn." For a few minutes he stood calling, but

again there was no answer. Instead he heard a
dog that sounded like Tandy yapping in the
distance. At once he plunged through the corn
in the direction of the yapping. Before long he
became certain that the yapping was coming
from Tandy.

At last he found Harry lying flat on his stomach watching Tandy and Bob play with a field

mouse. Tandy was barking at the mouse to cause it to scamper here and there. Bob was crouching, ready to pounce on it, if it came close enough.

At first, Grandpa Young was amused by this sight, but quickly his amusement gave way to anger. "Harry," he called, "jump up from there and come with me. We have been looking all over for you. It's almost dark and here you are about a half mile from the house. Surely you know better than to come so far out on the farm by yourself."

Back at the house Harry's mother gave him a good scolding, one he long remembered. She ordered him to play within calling distance of the house. Never again did he wander off on the big farm alone until he became old enough to go places safely by himself.

Caught Playing
in a Mudhole

"COME, VIV, let's race," said Harry. One hot summer day the boys were playing on the front porch. Often they raced from one end of the porch to the other. Usually Harry won because he was older and larger, but Vivian always seemed to like to race anyway.

"Good," replied Vivian. "I race."

The boys went to one end of the porch to line up. Soon Harry shouted, "Go!" and Vivian took off as rapidly as he could. Harry held back a little to give Vivian a fair chance. He didn't want him to become discouraged.

Just as Harry started to run, Tandy and Bob

23

came out of nowhere to join the race. They ran like a streak and Tandy came out ahead. "Tandy won the race," laughed Harry.

Moments later the boys had a great surprise. Their father, driving a team hitched to a wagon, returned from a trip to the nearby town of Grandview. "Whoa, Billy. Whoa, Tom," he called, as he pulled the horses to a stop.

The boys ran to greet their father. When they came near, he pulled out a little red wagon and said, "I've brought you a present."

"Oh, thank you, Papa," cried Harry, speaking for both himself and Vivian.

Moments later Harry picked up the handle of the wagon and said, "Climb in, Viv. Let me take you for a ride."

Promptly Vivian climbed into the wagon and pretended to drive. "Giddap, horsie," he called to Harry. "Giddap, horsie."

Before long a neighbor woman came to the

house to help Martha Truman with some sewing. She brought along her little son Chandler, who was about the same age as Vivian. When Chandler saw Harry and Vivian, he ran across the yard to play with them.

"Look," said Harry, pointing. "Papa just brought us a new wagon. I'm taking Viv for a ride. Come and climb in."

"In with Viv?" asked Chandler dubiously. "Can you pull me, too?"

"Sure," bragged Harry. "I can pull both of you. Just climb in and sit back of Viv in the wagon. Then I'll show you."

Chandler climbed into the wagon in back of Vivian, and Harry proudly started to pull them about the yard. Soon he opened a gate and pulled them along a lane in a large pasture by the barn. "I can't go very far," he said. "Mama ordered me to stay where she can call me."

He pulled the boys a short distance farther

until he came to a big maple tree. "Let's stop here to rest in the shade," he said. "Then I'll pull you back towards the barn."

Suddenly Tandy and Bob came running up to join the boys. Vivian and Chandler tried to put them into the wagon, but they kept jumping out. "They're afraid," called Harry. "They won't stay in the wagon by themselves."

"You come hold them," said Chandler. "We pull you in the wagon, too."

Harry laughed at this idea, but he climbed into the wagon and coaxed Tandy and Bob to join him. Then Vivian and Chandler tugged away to pull him and the two pets back along the lane to the barn. When they reached the barn, the two little boys threw themselves on the ground, completely exhausted.

While Vivian and Chandler rested, Harry tried to think of other ways to play with the wagon. Often he had heard Grandpa Young tell stories about big covered wagons being attacked by Indians in the West. Finally he said, "Let's play we're being attacked by Indians in the West. We'll be travelers in a big covered wagon and Tandy and Bob will be Indians."

"Oh, good," agreed the boys. "We play. You tell us what to do."

"Just watch out for Tandy and Bob," explained Harry. "Start to scream and call for help whenever they come near."

Vivian and Chandler climbed into the wagon, and Harry started to pull them back over the lane toward the big maple tree. Tandy and Bob ran along beside them, and every now and then Tandy took a nip at the wheels. Then Vivian and Chandler screamed and yelled, "Help! Indians come!"

Once when Tandy yelped, Harry started to run with the wagon as if trying to get away from the Indians. He neglected to watch where he was going and headed straight for a deep mudhole. He swerved, trying to avoid the hole, but dumped Vivian and Chandler into the sloppy mud. Both boys, taken by surprise, managed to crawl out, their clothes soaked with muddy water.

After the two boys recovered from fright, they begged Harry to let them pull him into the mudhole. Harry thought he could jump out to escape but landed in the mudhole, too. He scrambled to his feet and stepped out, covered with mud.

Now that all three boys were muddy and having fun, they decided to keep on playing here. Over and over again as they laughed and screamed, they took turns dumping themselves into the mudhole. They even put Tandy and Bob into the wagon and dumped them, too.

Later in the afternoon Martha and Chandler's mother decided to take a rest from their

sewing. When they stepped outside to saunter about the yard, they heard laughing and screaming in the distance. "Evidently the boys are having fun," said Martha. "Let's stroll out to see what they are doing."

On the way Martha told Chandler's mother about how Harry and Vivian enjoyed living on the big farm. "Everyday they seem to find something exciting to do," she said. "It's hard to tell what we'll find them doing today."

Moments later the two women spotted the three boys just as Harry was dumping Vivian and Chandler in the mudhole again. Martha was dumfounded. "Harry," she called, "I'm ashamed of you! All you boys and even Tandy and Bob are covered with mud."

Without waiting for an answer, Martha reached up and broke off a branch from a nearby tree. Quickly she stripped off the leaves and twigs to make a long switch. "Now, young man," she half-screamed, "march in front of me and pull that wagon back to the house!"

Bedraggled, mud-covered Harry started off slowly pulling the wagon. Every few steps his mother swished him across his legs with the long switch. Finally he stopped and started to explain. "First the wagon upset," he said. "We just fell in the mudhole."

"Don't try to explain," said his mother sternly. "We caught you playing in the mud. You are big enough to know better, but Vivian and Chandler are not. Remember from now on that you're supposed to help take care of little boys, not get them into trouble."

At this moment Harry wasn't very proud of being big enough to know better, as his mother had said. Back at the house all three boys had to scrub themselves in tubs of water and put on clean clothes. Martha loaned Chandler some of Vivian's clothes to wear home.

Christmas
in Summer

DURING THE summer months many persons came to the house on Grandpa Young's farm, some to visit and some to work. One morning Harry and Vivian were excited because their Uncle Harrison was coming. He was Mama's brother, who lived in Kansas City.

Uncle Harrison was coming to help with the chores while Grandpa Young attended the Cass County Fair. Grandpa was supposed to help judge the races at the fair.

Harry was looking forward to attending the fair, too. Grandpa Young had promised to take him along on the opening day. Uncle Harrison would do his chores in addition to his grandfather's chores while he was away.

Both Harry and Vivian were very fond of Uncle Harrison. He always found time to talk with them and to play with them. Often he brought them presents when he came to visit.

Early in the morning Mama came to the boys' bedroom and took some clean clothes from a closet shelf. "I'm getting out clean clothes for you to wear while Uncle Harrison is here today," she said. "Put them on while I go on downstairs to get breakfast."

Harry and Vivian hurried to get into their clean clothes. They rushed downstairs and washed their faces and hands. "You surely look neat," said Mama as she combed their hair. "Now sit down to eat breakfast."

The two boys took their places, and Mama put a fried egg, several slices of crisp fried bacon, a piece of toast, and a big helping of strawberry jam on each of their plates. Suddenly while Harry was eating, he asked, "Mama, was I named after Uncle Harrison? Is my real name Harrison, not just Harry?"

His mother answered slowly to make everything clear. "No, dear," she said. "Your real name is Harry, not Harrison. Your father and I are very fond of Uncle Harrison, but we really didn't name you after him."

Before Martha could explain further, Vivian asked, "How soon will Uncle Harrison come?"

"He may come anytime but probably not until this afternoon," replied his mother. "We'll just have to watch for him. It takes hours to drive here from Kansas City."

Nearly all morning Harry and Vivian stayed on the front porch watching for Uncle Harrison, but noon came and he still hadn't arrived. Finally, about the middle of the afternoon, Harry spotted his horse and buggy coming

34

down the road. "Mama," he shouted, "come fast! Uncle Harrison is almost here."

A few minutes later Uncle Harrison jumped down from his buggy. "Hello, Martha," he said, giving her a brotherly kiss. "How are my two favorite boys behaving these days?"

Quickly he reached down and picked Harry up in one arm and Vivian in the other. "You boys are getting so big that I can scarcely hold you any more," he said. Both boys started to hug him tightly around his neck. "Help, Martha," he cried. "They are choking me."

Harry and Vivian giggled at Uncle Harrison's little joke. Gently he put them down and said, "Now come and help me unload my parcels from the buggy. I have brought more than usual because I plan to stay several days. Your grandfather wants me to help with the chores."

"Yes, I know," said Harry. "He is going to the Cass County Fair. It starts tomorrow, and

I get to go with him. While we're away, you'll have to do both his chores and mine. Do you think you can do both our chores?"

Uncle Harrison was highly amused at Harry's serious question. He reached down, picked him up, and swung him high in the air. "Sure," he said. "I can do both your chores while you are away. Don't worry about them. Just go on to the fair and have fun."

"Thank you, Uncle Harrison," said Harry. "Afterwhile I'll show you what to do."

The excited boys started to help their uncle carry parcels into the house. "Here are two packages which we'll leave on the porch," he said. He pointed at two boxes which were wrapped neatly in bright colored paper.

After Uncle Harrison returned to the porch from carrying parcels into the house, he sat down in the porch swing. "Now, boys," he said. "You may open these boxes which we left here on the porch. The nearest box is for you, Harry, and the farthest box is for you, Vivian."

The boxes contained several gifts, all the same for both boys. Uncle Harrison always was very careful to treat both boys alike. First one boy and then the other pulled something out of his box and placed it on the floor. Each boy let out a cry of delight as he brought out something more. "This seems just like Christmas," exclaimed Harry. "Thank you, Uncle Harrison, for bringing all these things."

"Yes, thank you," echoed Vivian.

Harry started to call out his presents one by one. "Already I have a box of candy, a box of nuts, and a sack of oranges," he said.

"Me, too," echoed Vivian.

Soon Harry reached in his box and pulled out a strange-looking little red iron wagon with little iron horses pulling it and little iron men riding on it. He held it up curiously for Uncle

Harrison to see and called out, "What in the world is this wagon with horses and men?"

"That is a fire engine like the engines we have in Kansas City," explained Uncle Harrison. "The little men are firemen."

Harry jumped up and ran over to hug and kiss Uncle Harrison. Vivian jumped up and did the same. They now thought that they had one of the grandest uncles in the world.

Both boys started at once to play with their fire engines. Soon Harry discovered that he could remove the little iron firemen and horses from their places on his wagon. Vivian started to pull off his firemen and horses, too.

Soon both boys pretended that they were on their way to a fire. They knew little about fighting fires in a big city, but Uncle Harrison taught them how to play. "Clang, clang, clang," shouted Harry as he crawled on his knees to push the little red engine along.

"Clang, clang, clang," shouted Vivian, crawling on his knees close behind him.

Suddenly Grandma Young stepped out the door onto the porch and broke up the noisy game of fire fighting. She carried a big platter of sugar cookies. "Here, Harrison," she said. "Sample some of my fresh sugar cookies."

Harry rushed to get a sugar cookie, too. As he looked at Grandma Young, he thought of how lucky he was to have such a kind grandmother. Also, he thought of how lucky he was to have Grandpa Young, who was planning to take him to the Cass County Fair the next day.

Sometimes he wondered what his Grandmother Truman had been like. She had died long before he had been born. He well remembered his Grandfather Truman, however, as a friendly man who had died only two years before.

Soon Grandpa Young came around the corner of the house. He took off his straw hat, mopped his forehead with a big blue handkerchief, and shook hands with his son, Harrison. "Welcome home," he said. "I'm glad you could come to help with the chores while I attend the

Cass County Fair. Possibly Harry has told you that he is going with me tomorrow." Then glancing at the platter of cookies, he added, "Already your mother seems to be spoiling you with some of her fine baking, or maybe she's trying to bribe you so you will work hard at the chores."

"Oh, no!" cried Grandma Young. "Nobody needs to bribe Harrison to get him to work."

Grandpa Young smiled and went into the house to wash his hands. A few minutes later, he came back to the porch and sat down to visit. "Now I think I'll sample some of those good sugar cookies myself," he said.

Near evening Grandpa Young and Harry took Uncle Harrison on a trip to explain the chores, which he would have to do while they were away. Uncle Harrison listened carefully as Harry explained his part of the chores. These included helping to carry wood and water to the kitchen and helping to feed and water the chickens. Each afternoon he helped to gather the eggs.

That evening after supper all the grownups sat on the porch and talked about their plans for the next day. Harry sat off at one side to listen. He was careful not to interrupt, because he didn't want to miss any of the conversation. When his usual bedtime came, he wasn't the least bit sleepy. "Please let me stay up a little while longer," he begged.

"No," said his mother. "You have to go now. Remember that you'll have to get up extra early in the morning."

Slowly Harry climbed the stairs. Soon he found that he was sleepier than he had thought. He could still hear the grownups talking, but their voices lulled him to sleep.

Attending
the County Fair

THE NEXT MORNING Harry's mother called softly in his ear to awaken him. "Come, Harry," she said. "It's time to get ready to go to the Cass County Fair." Immediately Harry jumped out of bed, put on his Sunday clothes, and dashed downstairs to the kitchen.

Both Grandpa and Grandma Young were waiting for him in the kitchen. Grandma Young was busy frying bacon and eggs on the kitchen stove. She had arisen early to get breakfast for Grandpa Young and Harry.

Grandpa Young looked entirely different from the way he looked every day while working on the farm. He was dressed in his best Sunday clothes with a white handkerchief tucked in his breast pocket. His long flowing beard was neatly combed and trimmed.

Harry sat down at the table and began to gulp down his breakfast. "Slow down in your eating," cautioned Grandpa Young. "I don't want you to get sick on the way to the fair."

"Yes, there is no need to eat so fast," added Grandma Young. "Your grandfather won't go to the fair without you. Take time to pour some honey on your biscuit, but be careful not to spill any of it on your good clothes."

Grandpa Young ate slowly to get Harry to eat slowly. He talked about some of the interesting things they would see and do at the fair. Finally he arose from the table and walked around to pat his wife on the cheek. "Thank you, Harriet," he said, "for getting up early this morning to get breakfast for Harry and me."

After breakfast Grandpa Young went outside and hitched a horse to a two-wheeled cart. He pulled Harry up to the big seat beside him and started to drive away for Belton, where the fair would be held. Harry looked back and called, "Good-by," to his grandmother.

As Grandpa Young drove along the road to Belton, he talked almost constantly with Harry to keep him from becoming restless. Harry listened and talked, but wondered whether they ever would get there.

When they reached the fairground, Harry was careful to stay close to his grandfather but tried not to bother him. He realized that he shouldn't interfere with his grandfather's work. "Let's go directly to the grandstand," said Grandpa Young. "I want to talk with the other judges before the races begin. Besides, we'll be up high where we can watch the parade which will take place ahead of the races."

At the grandstand Grandpa Young met many persons whom he knew. Each time he proudly introduced Harry as his grandson. Finally he introduced him to Dr. Slaughter, one of the leading physicians in Belton. "Dr. Slaughter," he said, "I want you to meet my grandson, Harry S. Truman. We may need to call on you, if he eats too many sweets today."

"How do you do, sir," Harry responded politely, just as his mother had taught him.

"I'm proud to meet you, young man," replied Dr. Slaughter. "What are you planning to see here at the fair today?"

"I'm planning to see the parade and the horse races," replied Harry.

Grandpa Young led Harry to special seats in the grandstand which were reserved for the judges of the races. "We will watch the parade from up here," he said to Harry. "Before long it will start to come down the track."

A few minutes later three men riding beautiful prancing horses came down the track, followed by the Belton Brass Band. Next came a long string of horses and wagons. Each wagon had the name of some company or business person in Belton painted on the sides. It also had a demonstration or exhibit of some kind to advertise a certain type of business.

The first wagon had the name of a blacksmith painted on the sides. One man on the wagon was pounding a piece of iron, and two others were making a wagon wheel. "What are those men doing?" asked Harry.

"They are making a wagon wheel to show one of the many things people can get done at a blacksmith shop," replied Grandpa Young. "Blacksmithing is very important."

"Oh, look," cried Harry. "There comes a wagon with a tree in the center. How strange the tree looks. It has no leaves but it has animals hanging from the limbs. What does that wagon show with all those animals?"

"It is owned by a tanner in Belton," replied Grandpa Young. "He tans the hides of all the kinds of animals that you see hanging from the limbs of the tree."

Next came a wagon with a man putting a bridle and saddle on a horse. "That wagon is owned by a person who makes saddles and harnesses for horses," explained Grandpa Young.

One wagon was loaded with different kinds of furniture, including a bedstead, sofa, and all sorts of tables and chairs. "You don't need to tell me about this wagon," laughed Harry. "It is owned by a furniture store."

Another wagon contained a tall pyramid built of sacks of grain and flour. At the top of the pyramid was a sheaf of wheat. "That wagon may be hard for you to understand," said Grandpa Young. "It is owned by a milling company that grinds grain, such as wheat and corn, for farmers who live around Belton."

Still another wagon was loaded with lumber and products made from lumber, such as window frames and doors. At the back of the wagon was a huge saw and a planing machine. "That wagon belongs to the lumber mill here in Belton," said Grandpa Young. "It shows some of the products the mill can make."

The last entry in the parade demonstrated the importance of horses. A man was driving five teams of horses hitched to a farm wagon. Another man on the wagon was currying and brushing a horse. Fastened behind the wagon was a string of other vehicles, made up of two spring wagons and seven buggies. "My, that was a wonderful parade," exclaimed Harry.

"Yes," replied Grandpa Young. "Now someone will smooth the track to get it ready for the trotting horse races, which will come next."

Soon a man came down the track driving a horse hitched to a heavy wooden frame which smoothed out the hoof prints and wheel tracks left from the parade. The man went around the track several times to make sure that the track was perfectly smooth.

By now the grandstand was crowded with people waiting for the races to begin. Several men went here and there selling candy and peanuts to the crowd. Grandpa Young called to one of the men, "Bring us a bag of peanuts. This young man will need something to keep him busy while he watches the races."

In a few minutes the drivers began to bring their horses out on the track. Each horse pulled a high-wheeled cart, called a sulky. Each driver rode in a small seat on the sulky and kept tight lines on his horse.

Harry enjoyed watching his grandfather act as judge almost as much as he enjoyed watch-

ing the races. He wanted to remember different things that his grandfather did so he could
tell about them when he reached home. His
parents and Grandma Young would want to
know.

Harry was too young to understand all of his
grandfather's duties. The most that he could
tell was that he helped to decide which horses
came in first, second, and third in a race.

Spending this day with Grandpa Young at
the Cass County Fair was a great treat for
Harry. He found that Missouri farm folks, although they lived miles apart, could come together and hold a big celebration.

A New Sister
and New Glasses

HARRY, VIVIAN, and their two pets, Tandy and Bob, stretched out on the ground under a big maple tree in Grandpa Young's yard. "My, it's hot this morning," said Harry, fanning himself with a big palm-leaf fan. "I surely wish we could do something to cool off."

"Me, too," agreed Vivian. "And just look at poor Tandy and Bob."

"Yes," replied Harry. "Let's go to get a pan of cool water for them to drink. Grandpa Young says that August is one of the hottest months of the year here in Missouri."

Shortly after the boys brought the pan of

cool water to their pets, Grandma Young called to them from the kitchen door, "Come here, boys, I need you to help me."

The boys hurried into the kitchen wondering what their grandmother wanted. "I have a good cool job for you," she said. "Come to the cellar with me to help get a crockful of cabbage ready for making sauerkraut."

When the boys reached the cellar, she told them to sit on the bottom cellar step. Soon she placed a crockful of sliced cabbage and a big empty earthern jar in front of them. "Put the sliced cabbage into the jar slowly and tamp it down with this potato masher," she said, handing them a large wooden masher.

Grandma Young had asked the boys to help her mostly because she wanted to keep them busy. Early that morning their father had told them that their mother didn't feel well and that they shouldn't disturb her. He had stayed around the house in order to help take care of her. Later the doctor had come to the house to see her and he was with her now.

Both Harry and Vivian were worried about their mother. They couldn't understand why they weren't allowed to see her, and why the doctor had come. Finally Harry stopped tamping the cabbage and asked, "Why has the doctor come to see Mama? Is she real sick?"

"No, don't worry," replied Grandma Young. "Now that the doctor has come, I'm quite certain that she will be all right. Just keep on tamping away at the cabbage."

After these comforting words, the boys kept on taking the sliced cabbage from the crock and tamping it in the big earthern jar. They were thankful to be working for their grandmother in the cool cellar rather than trying to play out in the hot yard.

When the boys finished filling the big jar,

Harry asked, "Now, Grandma Young, what will you do with this jar of cabbage next? How will you make it into sauerkraut?"

Grandma Young started to explain how she would finish making sauerkraut from the cabbage. Right in the midst of her explanation, the boy's father came to the cellar door shouting, "We have a new baby girl!"

Their father came down the cellar steps and patted the boys on their heads. "You have a new baby sister," he said happily.

"May we go in to see her?" asked Harry.

"No, not for a while," replied his father. "Maybe after supper this evening you can go in to see her for a moment. Right now we must let her rest with Mama."

Minutes later Grandpa Young came to the kitchen. "Oh, Grandpa," cried Harry. "Viv and I have a new baby sister."

"What!" exclaimed Grandpa Young, giving

each boy a fond pat on the shoulder. "No wonder you're excited. I'm excited, too."

That evening Harry's father took him into the bedroom to see his new baby sister. "What's her name?" asked Harry excitedly.

"We plan to call her Mary Jane after your Grandmother Truman," replied his mother.

"I don't remember her," said Harry.

"No, she died before your father and I were married, but we both loved her," explained his mother. "Now we hope this tiny baby can become another Mary Jane Truman."

Harry gave his mother a big hug and turned to leave. "I'm glad about Mary Jane," he said. "Good night, Mama. I love you."

"I love you, too, Harry," said his mother. "Help Grandpa and Grandma Young all you can until I can take over my work again."

Harry obeyed his mother and tried to help his grandparents whenever possible. One morning Grandma Young said, "Our grapes are ripe. It's time to pick them to make jelly."

"Oh, good," exclaimed Harry. "I like grape jelly. What can I do to help you?"

"Well, I think you are old enough to do the picking," replied Grandpa Young. "You can fill baskets with grapes and bring them to your grandmother here in the kitchen."

Harry was happy and excited. "May I begin picking now?" he asked. Having his grandfather ask him to pick grapes made him feel very important. He felt almost grown-up.

"Sure," replied Grandpa Young. "Here are some small baskets which you may use for picking, and here is a box which you may stand on to reach some of the highest grapes."

He took Harry out to the big grape arbor back of the house. "Now let me tell you a few things about picking," he said. "Pick the grapes a bunch at a time. Take hold of each bunch and gently bend the stem back to break it loose from the vine. Then place the loose bunch carefully in the basket."

Harry tried to pick the grapes just as his grandfather had shown him. He carried one basketful after another to the kitchen. Finally he walked in proudly and said, "This is the last basketful I could find to pick. Now may I help you in the kitchen?"

"Of course," replied Grandma Young, "but first let me give you something to eat. You must be hungry after doing all that work." She placed a glass of milk and a slice of bread spread with strawberry jam on the table.

Harry mopped the perspiration from his forehead, washed his hands, and sat down at the kitchen table. While he was eating he became fascinated with the odor of grapes in the kitchen. "Always these days you're cooking something that smells good," he said.

Grandma Young smiled. "Well, this has been a fairly good year for growing certain kinds of fruits, including strawberries, apples, and grapes. Now I'm trying to put away all these kinds of fruits that I can for winter."

"Will we really eat all the jars of fruit that you are putting away?" asked Harry.

"Probably not," replied Grandma Young, "but we always need to look ahead. Some years are much better for growing certain fruits and vegetables than other years. Always we have plentiful years and lean years for growing things. During the plentiful years we need to save as much as we can for the lean years."

"I think I know what you mean," said Harry. "This has been a good year for strawberries, apples, and grapes. You're putting away all you can because next year may be a lean year."

"That's right," said his grandmother. "We never throw away extra fruits and vegetables.

Often when we have more than we need, we share them with some of our neighbors."

Harry was learning the ways of Missouri farm folks. The farmers lived far apart on their farms, but they tried to share with one another as much as possible.

During the coming weeks Harry spent much time helping his mother take care of his new baby sister, Mary Jane. Gradually his mother discovered, much to her surprise, that he had trouble seeing things. She noted, for instance, that he couldn't see various objects, such as a horse and buggy or even a tree or building, that she pointed out to him in the distance.

Already she had started to teach him to read, but mostly she had used the family Bible as a reader. The Bible had large printing, so she hadn't noted that his eyes were weak. Now, however, after she watched him moving about for several days, she became alarmed.

Finally one day she decided to take him to an eye doctor in Kansas City. When they reached the doctor's office, she explained, "My son can't see very well. Mostly he can't see things at a distance. I would like for you to examine his eyes and fit him with glasses."

The eye doctor glanced at Harry and asked him to sit in a big chair. He examined Harry's eyes by looking at them through a big magnifying glass. "Do your eyes hurt?" he asked.

"No," replied Harry. "They don't hurt. I just can't see things plainly."

"Well, I think I can fix you up so you can see better," said the eye doctor. "Just sit in this chair while I bring different pairs of glasses for you to try out. Then you can tell me which pair helps you to see best."

The eye doctor brought out a pair of glasses that were far too large for Harry to wear. The nose piece was so large and the bows were so

long that Harry had to hold the glasses to keep them on his head. "These glasses are far too big for me," he exclaimed. "I can't keep them on without holding them."

"I know," said the eye doctor. "Most glasses are made for adults. Very few children of your age wear glasses. Do the glasses help you to see any better?"

"No," said Harry, pulling the glasses from his head. "I can't see one bit better."

"Well, you probably need glasses with thick lenses," said the eye doctor. He brought out a pair of glasses with thick lenses to try. These glasses, however, like the others, had a big nose piece and long bows. Once more Harry had to hold them on with his hand, but he said, "I can see much better with these."

"Good," said the eye doctor. "Now let me get out one more pair for you to try. The next pair should be about right for you."

This time the eye doctor brought out a pair with still thicker lenses, but like the others, Harry had to hold them on his head. "Oh, these help me to see fine," he exclaimed, "but I can't keep them on."

"Don't worry," said the eye doctor. "I'll put together a pair that will fit you."

Carefully the eye doctor measured Harry's face to get the distance around his nose and the distance from his eyes to his ears. He went to a big case containing lenses and parts of frames, all of different sizes. With deft fingers he picked out and put together the lenses, nose piece, and bows which he thought were suited to Harry. "Here, try this pair on," he said, handing Harry the special pair which he had assembled. "I think they will fit you."

Harry put on the pair of glasses and was agreeably surprised by how comfortable they felt and by how well he could see. Suddenly he pulled them off and glanced at the lenses. "These glasses stay on my head and I can see well, but they are so heavy. Do I really have to wear thick glasses like these?"

"Yes, your eyes require thick glasses, and I'm afraid you'll have to wear them the rest of your life," said the eye doctor.

Harry slowly and soberly put the pair of glasses back on. "You'll just have to get used to wearing them," said his mother.

"That's right, and you'll have to be careful not to break them," said the eye doctor. "Don't play roughly with other children."

"I won't," promised Harry.

Harry's mother paid the eye doctor, and Harry wore his new glasses home. He was surprised by how many things he could see along the way. At home he delighted in telling Vivian how many new things he could see from the front porch.

Happy Times with a Pony

"THIS IS THE day we get my pony, get my pony, get my pony. This is the day we get my pony, early in the morning." Harry happily sang this little jingle in the morning as he rode along in the buggy with his father.

On Harry's sixth birthday a few weeks before, his father had promised to get him a Shetland pony as a birthday present. Now they were on their way to Belton to get the pony which his father had purchased. Harry was so excited that he could scarcely control himself. "Where will we find the pony?" he asked eagerly when they reached the village.

"We should find him hitched directly in front of the saddlery," replied his father. "The man was supposed to bring him there this morning from his farm."

Harry strained his eyes in the direction of the saddlery. Soon he caught a glimpse of a beautiful black pony hitched by the sidewalk in front of the building. "There he is!" he shouted, clapping his hands with joy. "There he is, right where you said he would be."

Moments later, when Harry's father drew near, Harry let out a deep sigh. "I guess this beautiful black pony isn't mine after all," he wailed. "He has a new leather saddle and my pony won't have any saddle. I'll have to use a blanket in riding my pony."

"No, you're wrong," said Harry's father. "Both the pony and the saddle are yours. I got you the saddle as a surprise. You won't need to use the blanket in riding him."

Harry walked over to the little black pony, held his head close to the pony's head, and patted him on the neck. He stroked the pony's mane and patted his right shoulder. Then the pony shook his head gently as if to say that he approved of Harry as a new friend.

After petting the pony, Harry started to admire the shiny new leather saddle with stirrups hanging down on both sides. Gingerly he put his left foot in the stirrup on the left side of the pony and pulled himself up. Then proudly he sat astride the pony with both feet in the stirrups. "You may sit there, if you wish, while I go inside to talk with the saddler for a few minutes," said his father. "Wait there until I come back."

John Truman chuckled at Harry's obvious happiness and went inside the saddlery. As Harry watched him, he thought, "How lucky I am to have such a fine father. Today he has made me one of the happiest boys in the world by buying me this pony and saddle."

Before long a man came walking along the sidewalk. When he noticed Harry, he paused and said, "How do you do, young man? Aren't you Solomon Young's grandson, and didn't you come here with him one summer to the Cass County Fair?"

Harry immediately recognized the man as one of his grandfather's friends whom he had met at the fair. "Yes, sir," he replied. "I'm Solomon Young's grandson and I came here with him one summer to the fair. I remember meeting you when you were helping to judge the races. Both you and Grandpa Young were judges."

Harry and the man were still talking about the fair when Harry's father came out of the saddlery. "Good morning, John," said the man. "How is everything going on the farm?"

"Fine, except that we are extremely busy right now," replied Harry's father. "Harry and I have come to town to get him a new pony and saddle. Now with a mount suited to his size, he'll make a good hand on the farm."

As Harry overheard these words, he held his head a little higher and sat a little straighter on the pony. He was pleased to know that his father had so much confidence in him, and he wanted to become a good helper.

A few minutes later it was time to start home. Harry's father unhitched the pony and handed Harry the reins. "You may try riding the pony for a few miles, and I'll follow along with the horse and buggy," he said.

Harry started off riding the pony along the streets of the village out into the country. Cautiously he watched the hard dirt road in front of him. He wanted to be sure that the new pony didn't step into any deep holes.

As Harry rode along proudly on the pony, he thought of how much fun he would have taking care of him from day to day. "I'll feed and water him, curry him, exercise him, and try to make him feel comfortable and happy living with us," he said to himself.

A few miles from town Harry and the pony came to a stream that flowed across the road. The pony would have to ford or wade across the stream because there was no bridge. Harry jumped off and led the pony to the edge of the stream to get a drink. The pony reached down his head and drank gratefully.

Harry's father pulled up beside the stream in his buggy. "You have been riding very well," he said, "but possibly from here on you should ride with me and give the pony a rest. Let's take off his saddle and put it in the buggy, and tie him to the back of the buggy. He'll welcome a chance to walk along behind and be free from carrying you and the saddle. Then you can ride him again after we get home."

Harry's father really thought that he had ridden far enough for the first time on his pony. He knew, however, that he would be better satisfied to ride in the buggy if he thought he was giving the pony a rest. Harry readily helped to remove the leather saddle from the pony's back and put it in the buggy. He helped to tie the pony to the back of the buggy with a long strap. "There, boy," he said. "We're going to give you a rest from here on."

When they reached home, Harry proudly displayed the pony and saddle to the other members of the family. His father helped him to put the saddle on the pony so he could ride about the yard. Afterward he helped Vivian to take a ride about the yard.

The next morning Harry arose early to ride his pony on an inspection trip about the farm.

After breakfast each morning, John Truman rode a horse over the big farm to inspect the fences and to make sure that the cattle and other farm animals were all right. Often Harry had accompanied him by riding ahead of him on the horse. Now he planned to accompany him by riding the pony.

Immediately after breakfast, Harry hurried to the barn to curry and bridle his pony. Moments later he called to his father, "I have my pony bridled, but you'll have to help me put on the saddle. From now on I won't have to ride on the same horse with you."

"No, and I'll be mighty glad to have you help me," said his father. "Grandpa Young and I have to keep watchful eyes in managing this big farm. Now that you have your new pony, you can be a big help to us."

"That's what I want," said Harry. "Let me help you all I can."

74

Harry's father riding a big horse and Harry riding his pony followed a lane leading to a big pasture in the farm. They rode slowly all the way around the pasture to look for possible breaks in the fences. They watched constantly for broken posts and broken barbed wire.

After they finished checking the fences, they rode close to the cattle, horses, and mules grazing in the pasture. "You look them over carefully to see whether any of them have been injured or seem to be ill," said Harry's father. "Then I'll count them to make sure all of them are here. As you see, we have to be very careful in raising animals."

"Yes, I know," replied Harry. "Animals need care just like people."

They rode to another pasture field, where more cattle were grazing. "Now we have a special job to do this morning," said Harry's father. "These are cattle which we are feeding for market, and some of them are already big and fat enough to sell. You can help me pick out the ones which seem to be ready."

Harry and his father sat in their saddles and picked out the biggest and fattest cattle in the herd. They drove these cattle off by themselves and formed a separate herd. Finally they drove this special herd along a lane to a pen near the barn. Harry had never felt prouder or happier in his life.

After this interesting experience, Harry was almost certain that he wanted to become a farmer. He tried hard to help his father and Grandpa Young in every way possible. He watched what they were doing, helped when he could, and tried to stay out of their way when he was too small to help.

One evening he was thrilled when his father announced that the time had come to thresh wheat. "The threshing crew will come tomorrow with the steam engine and the threshing machine," he explained. "Our neighbors in the threshing ring will come with their horses and wagons to help us. We probably will have a dozen extra men here for dinner. It will take about three days to thresh all the wheat."

At once Harry knew what the threshing work would be like. He remembered about the various activities from the years before. Already, hired men had cut the wheat in the fields with a binder which had bound it into bundles or sheaves. Afterwards they had picked up the bundles and put them in shocks. Now neighbors would come to haul the bundles to the threshing machine.

The farmers of the neighborhood had formed a group, called a threshing ring, to help one another during the threshing season. They followed the threshing machine from farm to farm and helped to carry on the different kinds of

work which needed to be done. By helping one
another, all of them got their grain threshed
promptly without hiring extra helpers.

Early the next morning the steam engine and

threshing machine arrived at Grandpa Young's farm. Harry and Vivian stood off to one side to watch as the steam engine went puffing by the house toward the barn.

Harry could readily see that this would be a busy day on the farm. "Mama," he said, "I'll be your wood and water boy today while the threshers are here. I've already filled the wood box with sticks from the wood pile and will bring more when you need them. Also I've filled the reservoir with water and brought an extra bucketful for you to use."

A few minutes later Grandpa Young asked him to help prepare drinking water to take to the men in the fields. "Here are six big jugs," he said. "Fill them with water as cold as you can get from the well. Then put cold water on the burlap wrappers around the jugs."

Harry carefully filled the jugs with cold water and wet the wrappers with cold water. He helped Grandpa Young load the jugs of water onto a wagon. Then he watched him drive away to take the drinking water to the men.

A day or so later while the threshers were still at Grandpa Young's farm, Harry used his pony to carry water to the men. He tied a jug of water on each side of the pony's saddle and led the pony to the fields.

Even though Harry was busy, he found time to watch the threshing machine work. Men brought wagons loaded with bundles of wheat from the fields and tossed them into the front of the machine. Then the machine poured tiny kernels of wheat out of a spout at one side and tossed the stalks or straw out the back. Men worked to put the kernels of wheat into big bags and other men worked with pitchforks to build a big stack out of the straw.

A couple of months later when Harry arose one morning to close his bedroom window, he noticed that everything outside was covered with frost. "Brrr, it must be cold out there this morning," he said to himself as he pulled down the sash. "Winter will soon be here."

A few minutes later he sat down to eat breakfast with his father and Grandpa Young. "We're going to butcher hogs today," said his father. "Your grandmother will need you and Vivian to help her in the kitchen."

"Oh, good," said Harry.

After breakfast Grandma Young started to wash, dry, and put away the dishes. Moments later she placed on the table a big crock partially filled with a mixture of salt and sugar and two cups partly filled with black pepper and cayenne pepper. "Now, Harry," she said, "pour these cups of pepper slowly into the jar and mix the pepper with the salt and sugar. Handle the pepper carefully to avoid getting some of it in your nose and eyes."

"I'll be very careful," said Harry. "I already know what it can do to me."

A short time later Harry's father brought in a big tub filled with two hams, two shoulders, and two pieces of side meat from a newly butchered hog. He took out all these big chunks of meat and placed them on the kitchen table. Then Grandma Young showed Harry and Vivian how to rub the salt, sugar, and pepper mixture into the different chunks to get them ready for the smokehouse. The two boys rubbed and rubbed. Finally Vivian looked up and asked, "Have we rubbed enough?"

Grandma laughed. "You can't get tired yet," she said. "We still have to do the meat from two more hogs."

"Then we'll still have to do four more hams, four more shoulders, and four more pieces of side meat," said Harry.

"That's right," said Grandma Young. "Suppose you rest for a while until your father brings in the meat from the next hog. Wash your hands and I'll give you some cookies and milk while you are waiting and resting."

While the boys ate, they talked about the good ham and bacon which they would have to eat later. "Will we get any sausage or pickled pigs' feet from the hogs?" asked Harry.

"Oh, yes," replied Grandma Young, "but we can't do everything at once. We'll prepare the sausage and pickled pigs' feet later."

The work went on hour after hour. Everyone in the family had a share in preserving the meat for the winter. Later the hams, shoulders, and pieces of side meat would be put into the smokehouse in the back yard, where they would be smoked for several weeks.

That afternoon Grandma Young brought out a board covered with chunks of white fat meat, which she had trimmed from the hogs. "Here,

Harry," she said. "I believe you are old enough to help cut up these chunks of fat meat for making lard. Take this paring knife and cut them into as fine pieces as you can."

Harry carefully cut the chunks of fat meat into small pieces for making lard. He felt very proud to be trusted to do this important work. Grandma Young was proud of him, too.

As Harry worked, his father pulled out the hearts and livers from a tub. Grandma Young asked him to get some liver ready to fry for supper. She felt that fried liver would taste good after the hard day's work.

Harry was curious when Grandpa Young brought in the heads of three hogs and tossed them into a huge kettle on the stove. "What will we make out of them?" he asked.

Grandpa Young started to laugh. "When we Missouri farm folks butcher a hog for the winter, we save everything but the squeal," he said.

A New Home
in Independence

In December, 1890, John Truman and his family moved from Grandpa Young's farm to a home of their own on South Crysler Street in Independence, Missouri. This home, even though it was in town, was somewhat like a small farm. It had a barn and enough land for planting a garden and keeping several farm animals. Harry's father allowed him to bring his black Shetland pony and soon bought him and Vivian a pair of goats with harness and wagon.

Independence was only a few miles from Kansas City, the largest city in the western part of the state. Many people of Independence worked there, traded at big stores there, and went there to attend important events.

One day in the early spring, Harry said to Vivian, "I'm beginning to like living here in Independence. When Papa first talked about moving here, I was afraid we would live on a crowded lot with no room to plant things or to keep farm animals. Now it seems almost the same as living in the country."

"That's right," said Vivian, "only we have fewer chores and more time to play."

"Yes," said Harry. "I'm surely glad that Papa let me bring my pony along and that he bought us the two goats with harness and wagon. Now we can always find ways to have fun."

One Saturday in early June the boys' mother asked them to take a bucket and go to the strawberry patch to pick strawberries for Sunday dinner. "Don't eat so many while you are picking them that there won't be any left for dinner," she said jokingly. "I want to be sure to have plenty to go around."

The boys enjoyed picking the big strawberries and putting them into a bucket. Every now and then they paused long enough to tuck a berry or two in their mouths, but most of the time they kept busy filling the bucket. "Let's hurry so we can hitch up the two goats and take a ride," said Harry.

"Maybe we can take Mary Jane for a ride," said Vivian. "She's nearly two years old and big enough to go riding with us."

"We'll ask Mama," said Harry.

"Of course," said Vivian, "and we'll promise to take good care of her."

A short time later the boys took the bucket of strawberries to the house. "Oh, good!" said their mother. "Now I'll clean them and put them away for dinner tomorrow."

While the boys were resting, they asked,

"May we take Mary Jane riding with our goats and wagon? We'll be very careful to keep her from getting hurt."

"Yes, but don't go outside the yard," cautioned their mother.

The boys ran to the barn and soon came back driving their goats. They stopped at the back door to pick up Mary Jane and drove her all about the yard. She laughed and screamed with joy as she rode with the boys.

Now that Harry had fewer chores to do in Independence, he began to take a special interest in reading. Each day he took down the big family Bible and tried to read some of the passages. He now could make out many words by himself and his mother helped him to recognize the words that were too difficult for him.

The Trumans found it much easier to attend church in Independence than when they had lived on Grandpa Young's farm. They decided to attend the First Presbyterian Church only a few blocks from their home. "The denomination doesn't matter," said Mrs. Truman. "All churches worship the same God. If we go to church nearby, we're more likely to attend regularly than if we go to church farther away."

The first day Mrs. Truman took the children to Sunday School, Harry wasn't particularly happy about going. He was timid about meeting people and didn't want them staring at him. Besides, he knew that all the people at the church would be strangers.

When they reached the door of the church, a leader stepped forward to greet them. Mrs. Truman explained to him that they were newcomers in Independence and that they wished to attend services at this church. "We'll be very pleased to have you," he said.

There was only one big meeting room in the church. All the Sunday School classes met in different parts of the room. After the Sunday School ended, the preaching services would be held in the same room. There were three classes for young people in the Sunday School, one for little children, one for middle-age children, and one for teen-agers. There were two classes for adults, one for men and one for women. Already these classes could be seen seated here and there in different groups, waiting for the Sunday School to start.

The church leader took Mrs. Truman to the class for women and introduced her to the teacher. The teacher, in turn, introduced her to the women in the group. All extended her a hearty welcome as a new member.

Next, the leader took Harry and Vivian to the class for middle-age children and introduced them to the teacher. "Welcome, Harry and Vivian," said the teacher, escorting them to a couple of empty seats at the back.

90

Minutes later, the superintendent of the Sunday School stepped up to the pulpit to start the services. "Let's open our Sunday School this morning by singing that old familiar hymn, 'Blest Be the Tie That Binds,' Number 68 in the hymnal. Please stand while we sing."

Harry and Vivian quickly found the song in the hymnal and listened as the organ started to

play. They could see the organist well and curiously watched him move his hands and feet. As he played Harry became so interested in watching the organist that he almost neglected to sing when the time came. Finally he managed to join with the others in singing the following lines:

"Blest be the tie that binds
Our hearts in Christian love.
The fellowship of kindred minds
Is like to that above."

Moments later, while Harry was singing other lines in the song, he happened to notice a girl with beautiful golden curls directly in front of him. He watched her so closely that he lost his place in the songbook and had trouble reading the words.

After the singing and a prayer, the teachers took charge of the classes. The teacher of the middle-age children introduced Harry and Vivian to the other members of the class. "Boys and girls," she said, "we have two new friends to join us this morning, Harry and Vivian Truman. Now will each of you in turn introduce yourself and welcome them to the class."

Harry wanted to run away and hide, but he felt braver when he heard how shyly some of the boys and girls spoke. He nodded politely and muttered a soft "How do you do?" as each child spoke to him.

Finally the girl with the golden curls stepped up to welcome him. "I'm Elizabeth Virginia Wallace," she said, "but most folks call me Bess instead of Elizabeth."

As Harry looked at this girl, he noticed that she not only had golden curls but also sparkling blue eyes. He was so stunned by her looks that he neglected to say, "How do you do?" From that time on, he had a reason for wanting to attend Sunday School in Independence.

Beginning School Days

DURING THE first two years after the Truman family moved to Independence, Harry's mother continued to teach him at home. He learned to read and write well under her direction. With his new glasses, he could readily see the print in books and newspapers.

When he was eight years old, his mother decided to send him to school so that he could study with other children. He would have to start as a beginner, but she felt that he would advance rapidly. He would have an advantage because he already could read and write.

On the first day he walked to Noland School

all by himself. As he walked along, he wondered what the teacher would be like and what the pupils would be like. He felt confident because he was eager to learn.

After he reached the building, he inquired for the beginners' room. When he entered the door, the teacher greeted him and led him to an empty seat. Other children were standing in groups here and there talking and laughing, but most of them were strangers to him. Soon a loud bell sounded outside in the hall, calling all the rooms to order.

All the children sat down in their seats and looked toward the front of the room. The teacher arose from her desk and said pleasantly, "Boys and girls, my name is Miss Ewing. I'm pleased to welcome you on your first day of school. First, we'll get acquainted so that we can work and play together during the year.

"Now," she added, as she held up a book, "I

need to ask all of you for your names so I can write them in this roll book. Then I'll give pencils and paper to all of you who can write so you can write the names, too. How many of you know how to write?"

Harry and two other pupils held up their hands. Miss Ewing handed three pencils and three sheets of paper to them. She smiled as she handed both pencil and paper to Harry.

The pupils started to give their names one after another, and Miss Ewing spelled them out for Harry and the two other pupils who were writing. Soon it was Harry's turn to give his name. "My name is Harry S. Truman," he said bravely.

Miss Ewing spelled out the name Harry. Then she paused and asked, "What middle name does the initial S stand for? We need your full middle name for our records. What were you christened when you were born?"

"My middle name is just a capital "S" with a period after it," explained Harry. "I really don't have a middle name."

"I don't understand," said Miss Ewing. "Surely the letter "S" stands for a name."

"No," replied Harry. "When I was born, my parents couldn't decide whether to call me Shippe after my Grandfather Truman, or Solomon after my Grandfather Young."

"Well, that certainly is a very unusual situation," said Miss Ewing. "I guess we'll just have to write down your middle name as capital 'S' with a period after it."

Harry liked school and found his work very interesting. As his mother anticipated, he applied himself and made rapid strides in his studies. His one big problem was that he couldn't play actively with the other pupils during the recesses because of his glasses.

Often at recess, when the children played

rough-and-tumble games, he merely stood beside the building and watched them. He only played with them when their games required little moving about. One day while he was standing by the building watching the other pupils, Miss Ewing came by and said, "I'm sorry that you can't be out here playing. Is there anything I can do to help you?"

"Oh, no, Miss Ewing," replied Harry. "Thank you for asking, but I don't mind standing here and watching. As a matter of fact, I'm beginning to enjoy it."

Miss Ewing noticed that Harry hadn't complained about wearing glasses. She understood, because she realized that he probably would have to continue wearing them for the rest of his life. For this reason he needed to learn to cope with the problem.

Usually at recess some of the pupils played a game of baseball. One day Harry noticed that the boy who usually umpired their games was absent from school. When recess came he bravely walked over to the players and asked, "May I serve as your umpire today?"

"Have you ever played baseball?" asked the players. "You never play here with us. Are you sure that you know the rules of the game?"

"Just try me," urged Harry. "If I don't umpire to suit you, I'll readily quit."

Harry soon demonstrated that he knew the rules well, and all the players were pleased with his decisions. Miss Ewing watched him closely from one of the classroom windows. She was pleased to see how ably he assumed responsibility.

During this year of 1892 Harry not only started school, but he started to become interested in politics. That was the year for holding a Presidential election. Benjamin Harrison, a Republican, who had been elected four years before, was running for re-election, and Grover Cleveland, a Democrat, was running against him. John Truman was a strong Democrat, who urged all his neighbors and friends to vote for Grover Cleveland.

Harry, who became almost as excited about the election as his father, read all the newspaper articles possible about Harrison and Cleveland. One day he said, "Papa, I just read an article which calls Cleveland a 'perpetual candidate.' What does the word perpetual mean?"

"It means continuous or everlasting," said his father. "Your mother has taught you the names of all the Presidents with the dates when they served. If you'll think back over the names of the latest Presidents, you probably will understand why the article calls Cleveland a perpetual candidate."

Harry thought briefly and said, "Grover Cleveland was the twenty-second President.

He was elected in 1884 and served from 1885 to 1889. Benjamin Harrison was the twenty-third President, elected in 1888. He took office in 1889 and his term will end in 1893. Cleveland must have been President when Harrison was elected four years ago. Did Cleveland run for re-election while he was President?"

"Yes, but he was defeated by Harrison," replied Mr. Truman.

"Now I understand what the article means," said Harry. "This is the third time that Cleveland has run for President."

"That's right," said Mr. Truman. "I voted for him four years ago, and I am going to vote for him again this fall."

On election day Harry's father was very busy urging others to vote for Grover Cleveland. The next morning when Harry left for school, nobody knew whether Harrison had been re-elected or whether Cleveland had defeated him. A day or so later, however, after all the votes had been counted, the news came that Cleveland had won.

That afternoon when Harry returned home from school, he found his father moving about on the roof of the house. "Papa, what are you doing up there?" he asked curiously.

"Just stand where you are and you'll find out," replied his father.

Mr. Truman wrapped colored cloth around the wooden support of a weathervane on the house. Then he put up a big United States flag that waved and flapped gracefully in the breeze. When he climbed down from the roof, he grabbed Harry by the shoulders and started to dance him round and round. "What in the world is going on?" asked Harry.

"We Democrats are beginning to celebrate," his father said, "because Grover Cleveland has been elected President. Tonight we plan to have a big torchlight parade along the streets of Independence. This will be one of the biggest parades ever held in the city. Everybody will turn out to see it."

"May I go to the torchlight parade?" asked Harry eagerly. "I want to watch you celebrate your Democratic victory."

"Why, certainly you may go to the parade," replied his father. "I want you to see how we Democrats can celebrate. Just find a good place to stand and watch."

That night Harry proudly stood close by a street to watch the Democratic victory parade. First came a band, playing loud and gay marching music. Next came a wagon displaying huge pictures of Grover Cleveland and Adlai F. Stevenson, the newly-elected President and Vice-President. As Harry looked, he wondered whether he would ever get to see a President or Vice-President in person.

Several prominent local Democratic officials rode in the wagon with the pictures. Immediately behind this wagon came Harry's father and numerous other men riding horses draped with red, white, and blue bunting. Harry proudly waved and called to his father as he rode by. Last came hundreds of persons carrying torches and singing patriotic songs.

Harry was only eight years old, but he was fascinated with this political celebration. It helped him to realize how fortunate he was to live in a country where people could choose their own leaders. From now on he was determined to learn as much as possible about our country and system of government.

First in his search for information he tried to find out as much about Grover Cleveland as he could. He read several stories about him in books and newspapers and came to look upon him as one of his favorite heroes.

Seriously Ill
with Diphtheria

"Mama, I'm not hungry this morning," said Harry, pushing his plate of scrambled eggs and sausage to one side. He had just come down to eat breakfast before starting to school. Usually he had a good appetite and ate a hearty breakfast before leaving.

Both his father and mother looked at him in surprise. "Well, you'll either have to eat or stay here at home today," said his mother. "You can't go to school on an empty stomach."

Above everything else Harry didn't want to stay at home. He was advancing rapidly in his studies and was very proud of his record. Halfheartedly he pulled the plate back in front of him and started to pick away at the food. He had to force down every bite, but he kept on picking away until he managed to clean the plate. Finally he arose from the table and got ready to take off for school.

It now was mid-winter, and his mother reminded him to dress warmly because it was cold and snowy outdoors. As he trudged along the street, he shivered as he had never shivered before. Usually he enjoyed walking in the cold, but this morning he could hardly wait to reach the warm school building.

All forenoon he sat slumped in his seat, with aches and pains shooting through his body. He tried to study but couldn't think well, and he couldn't recite well in class. All forenoon he wished that he could stretch out somewhere and go to sleep.

Several times during the day the teacher,

Miss Minnie Ward, noticed that he was acting strangely. About mid-afternoon she walked back to his desk to talk with him. "Don't you feel well today, Harry?" she asked anxiously. "You've been sitting slumped in your seat and don't seem to be as alert as usual."

"No, Miss Ward," replied Harry. "I guess I should have stayed at home today because I don't feel like studying. Now I'm just sitting here waiting for the time to go home."

"Well, it isn't time for school to close yet, but you can leave any time now," said Miss Ward. "I'll write a note, explaining that you don't feel well, for you to take home to your mother. Then she won't think that you got into some kind of trouble here at school."

Both Harry and Miss Ward chuckled at this little joke, and Miss Ward went back to her desk to write the note to Harry's mother. Moments later she handed him the note and asked, "Do you feel like going home by yourself? If not, I'll get someone to go with you."

"Oh, no," replied Harry. "Don't worry about me. I'll get there all right."

"In case you don't feel better by tomorrow, I suggest that you stay at home," said Miss Ward. "You may be getting some contagious disease and expose the other children."

"All right, Miss Ward," said Harry. "I hadn't thought about exposing the other children. I'll stay at home if I don't feel better."

Harry left the school building and started to drag his feet wearily through the snow. As he trudged along, he felt occasional tears trickling down his cheeks. Some of these tears came from exposure to the bitter-cold weather, some from his sick-ridden body, and some from the idea of having to miss school.

When Harry, exhausted and dejected, finally reached home, his mother realized at once that he was ill. "You're sick," she said anxiously. "I can tell just by looking at you. This morning I was afraid you didn't feel well when you forced yourself to eat breakfast so you could go to school."

"Yes, but now I'm sorry that I went," replied Harry. "I've felt sick all day and finally Miss Ward sent me home. She wrote you this note to explain why she sent me."

His mother read the note quickly and placed it on the table. "I'm glad Miss Ward sent you home early," she said. "Now we can begin to look after you. I'll ring the bell to call your father to the house. Then he can go to get a doctor to come to see you. Possibly you're getting some kind of contagious disease and the sooner we find out, the better."

Harry's mother went to the kitchen door and rang a big hand bell. A few minutes later his father came rushing into the room. "Why did you call me?" he said anxiously. "Is something wrong here at the house?"

"Yes, Harry has come home sick from school," replied Mrs. Truman, "and we should arrange for a doctor to see him. Jump on a horse and go to call a doctor. Then when you come back, perhaps you should take Mary Jane to stay with Grandma Young. We don't want her to risk catching some kind of contagious disease from Harry."

Since the Trumans had moved to Independence, Grandpa Young had died, but Grandma Young still lived on the big farm. Often Mrs. Truman took Harry, Vivian, and Mary Jane to stay with her for a few days.

By the time the doctor came, Harry had developed a high fever and a sore throat. The doctor examined him carefully, but couldn't decide at first what was wrong with him. He came back to see him every few hours and finally decided that he had diphtheria, a dangerous infection of the throat.

At that time people feared diphtheria as one of the worst diseases in existence. No means of preventing or curing it had yet been discovered. As a result, it attacked a great many children and often proved fatal.

Four days after Harry became ill, Vivian came down with the same disease. Their mother waited on the two boys constantly, both day and night. She fanned them and placed cold wet cloths on their foreheads to try to reduce their fever. She placed hot poultices on their throats to help reduce congestion.

It was almost impossible to get her to leave the boys' room. Her husband prepared meals, but she completely lost interest in food. "Martha," he said, "come and eat something. We can't allow you to get sick, too."

"I feel all right," replied Martha, "but I'm

not hungry and I won't be so long as our two little boys are lying here seriously ill. I just can't leave them, even for a minute."

During the next few days Vivian started to improve and soon made a complete recovery. Harry, on the other hand, developed complications and had to remain flat on his back in bed. The diphtheria left him paralyzed so that he could neither speak nor move his arms and legs. He had to eat mostly liquid foods, because he couldn't swallow well. His mother had to feed him whenever he ate.

Even though Harry was paralyzed, his mind was perfectly alert and he could see and hear well. His favorite pastime while he was paralyzed was listening to his mother read. Hour after hour she sat beside him and read his favorite stories and books. Some of them he wanted her to read over and over again.

After several weeks he began to regain the

use of his muscles. Gradually he recovered the ability to speak and to move about again. He improved so slowly, however, that his school closed for the summer before he was able to leave the house. "What am I going to do about my work, Mama?" he asked. "I have missed the whole last half of the second grade."

"Don't worry," comforted his mother. "After you gain a little more strength, you can begin to study again. At first, I'll help you and maybe later you can go to summer school."

Soon Harry's mother got out his books and helped him go over the work which he had missed. Before long she arranged for him to attend summer school at the Columbian School. After a few days the teacher, Miss Jennie Clements, said to him, "Harry, you already are ahead of your class and actually don't have any work to make up. Why not study some advanced work so you can join a higher class?"

"Do you mean that if I study harder books I might be promoted to a higher class?"

"Yes, that's exactly what I mean," replied Miss Clements. "Would you like to try?"

"Of course," replied Harry. "Please let me know what books my parents will need to buy for me so I can get started. I can't play much yet, so I'll have plenty of time to study."

Harry's parents gladly purchased the necessary books and he began to study. He was so thrilled that he could scarcely put the books aside long enough to eat and sleep. He studied them from cover to cover.

All the while Miss Clements provided helpful guidance at school. Near the end of the summer she gave him oral and written examinations, which he readily passed. "Congratulations, Harry," she said. "You have thoroughly mastered the advance work. This fall I'll arrange for you to join a new group at school."

116

That fall Harry attended the Columbian School where he joined a group of pupils approximately his own age. Although he hadn't started school until he was eight years old and had missed one half year because of illness, he now was with the class where he really belonged. Most of the pupils would continue to be his classmates on through elementary school and high school. One was Bess Wallace, the girl with the golden curls and sparkling blue eyes, whom he had met in Sunday School a few years before.

The Waldo
Avenue Gang

SOON AFTER Harry recovered from his serious illness, the Trumans moved to a home on Waldo Avenue in Independence. This home, like their former home, had a barn and enough land for raising a garden and keeping a few animals, including the black Shetland pony and a pair of goats. There was a big yard in front of the house and a big fenced-in yard, or small field, next to the barn at the back, where the animals could be turned loose to get exercise.

The Trumans had several nearby neighbors on Waldo Avenue, some of whom had children about the same ages as the Truman children.

Almost immediately these children began to come to the Truman house to play, either in the front yard or in the fenced-in yard at the back. Sometimes they played with the black Shetland pony or the pair of goats, and at other times they played games.

Gradually as the children played together repeatedly, they began to call themselves the Waldo Avenue Gang. Most of the time Harry, who was one of the oldest members of the group, acted as leader. He helped the others to get along well together.

One of Harry's favorite friends in the Waldo Avenue Gang was Bess Wallace, who lived only a short distance away and was one of his classmates in school. Bess had a brother, named Frank, who also was a member of the gang and one of Harry's favorite friends.

Even though the children in the gang knew one another well, they were almost strangers to

Harry's mother. She knew most of their faces but couldn't call them by name. Usually they played outside in the yard, so she had little opportunity to meet them.

One summer afternoon after she had just finished baking a batch of cookies, she looked out the back door and saw Harry and Vivian giving the children rides with their goats and wagon. Suddenly she decided that this would be a good time to get better acquainted with the children. "Stop playing for a few minutes and come into the house to get some cookies and milk," she called to them.

The children promptly streamed into the kitchen. "Welcome to you," said Mrs. Truman. "Some of you are almost strangers to me and I want to get better acquainted with you. Please step forward and give me your names, one by one, so I can fit them with your faces."

"You heard what my mother requested,"

called Harry. "The price of two cookies and a glass of milk will be to tell her your name."

The children courteously formed a line at the kitchen table. Each child in turn stepped up to the table, gave his name, thanked Mrs. Truman, and picked up his cookies and milk. The first child, with polite manners and words, set the pattern for all the others. "I'm Jim Wright," he said. "Thank you."

Then all the other children followed suit by saying, one after another:

"I'm Frank Wallace. Thank you."

"I'm Bess Wallace. Thank you."

"I'm Bernard Pittman. Thank you."

"I'm Paul Bryant. Thank you."

"I'm Harry Truman. Thank you."

"I'm Vivian Truman. Thank you."

"I'm Mary Jane Truman. Thank you."

All the neighbor children laughed when the Truman children stepped up and introduced themselves to their mother. Mrs. Truman laughed along with the others.

"Let's go out to the back yard to eat," said Harry, thinking of the crumbs that his mother would have to sweep up from the kitchen floor. He started to lead the way.

"Good-by, Mrs. Truman, you surely have been good to feed us this afternoon," called Frank Wallace as he turned to follow.

"Yes, good-by, Mrs. Truman," chorused the others as they trooped out the door.

"Good-by, and thanks for telling me your names," called Mrs. Truman.

Harry took the children to a big tree where they could eat in the shade. While they were relaxing, they talked about how much room the Truman children had for playing. "Yes, we're lucky to have plenty of room, and we're lucky to have all you friends to come to play with us," said Harry. "What do you want to play

122

from now on this afternoon? We might as well try to decide while we're resting."

"I would like to keep on playing with the goats and wagon," said Jim Wright. "You and Vivian are my only friends who have goats."

"I would like to play with your black pony," said Frank Wallace. "You are my only friend who has a pony."

"Let's play pigtail baseball," said Paul Bryant. "Then we can all play together at once and not have to take turns."

"I guess we'll have to take a vote to decide," said Harry. "All in favor of continuing to play with the goats and wagon hold up your hands. I see only two hands being held up.

"All in favor of playing with my pony hold up your hands," Harry continued. "I see only one hand being held up. Evidently most of you want to play pigtail baseball."

"Hurrah!" shouted all the children who had

wanted to play baseball. "We win! We get to play baseball."

"That's all right," cried the others. "We'll gladly play baseball with you."

"You'll have to give me time to put the goats away before we begin to play," said Harry. "I can't leave them standing here hitched to the wagon the rest of the afternoon."

"I'll go along to help you," cried Frank Wallace, climbing into the wagon behind Harry.

Harry drove the goats to the barn, where Frank jumped out and opened the barn door. Then he and Harry unfastened the harness and hung it on large wooden pegs. The goats willingly went in their pen, happy to be there.

When Harry and Frank returned from unhitching the goats, the other children said, "Harry, we want you to be umpire. Help us to choose positions so we can start to play."

"Well," said Harry, "it's fairly late in the

afternoon, so we'll only have about an hour to play. Then we'll have to quit playing to start doing our evening chores."

Pigtail baseball was quite different from ordinary baseball. There was just one long string of players trying to work their way up to the batting position. Whenever a new batter was needed, each player advanced his position, as from shortstop to pitcher, pitcher to catcher, catcher to batter. All players tried to get the batters out so they could advance.

In starting a game there always was the problem of determining who would fill different playing positions, as who would be pitcher and who would be catcher. Usually the positions were determined by some method of choosing up.

Harry held up a baseball bat and said, "All of you start at the bottom and grip this bat with your right hands directly above one another. Then from there on up, grip it with your left hands, one after the other. The last person who is able to grip the bat will get to choose first. We'll let the girls grip first."

The children followed Harry's orders. All the children gripped the bat with their right hands and then started to grip it with their left hands. Frank Wallace was the last person to be able to grip the bat. "I get first choice," he cried. "I choose to be batter."

Next the children gripped the bat to find out who would be catcher, pitcher, shortstop, basemen, and fielders. Bernard Pittman was the first catcher, Vivian Truman the first pitcher, and Bess Wallace the first shortstop. The others were basemen and fielders, but there weren't enough to fill all the positions.

The game immediately got under way with Harry acting as umpire. Vivian threw his first pitch straight across the plate to catcher Bernard Pittman for a strike. He threw again, but this time Frank Wallace hit the ball and sent it into center field. Jim Wright, who was playing fielder, chased the ball and threw it to Paul Bryant, who was covering second base. In the meantime Frank Wallace had rounded first base and reached second base standing up. He was standing on the base when Paul Bryant caught the ball.

"Safe at second base!" called Umpire Harry. "Batter up! Catcher Pittman, advance to batter. Every player move up one position."

The players had to move up because they had failed to get Frank Wallace out and needed another batter. Vivian, who had just been pitcher, now became catcher, and Bess Wallace, who had been shortstop, now became pitcher. As Bess took over her position, Harry noticed once again how pretty she was with her golden curls and sparkling blue eyes.

Bess was not only a beautiful girl, but she also was a good baseball player. She threw three successive strikes across the plate to put batter Pittman out. "Batter out," called Umpire Harry. "All players move up one position from where you were playing."

The game went on in this manner with everybody having fun until Umpire Harry decided that it was time to stop playing. The members of the Waldo Avenue Gang always had fun when they came to the yard to play.

Work Comes First

"HARRY, IT'S five o'clock," his mother whispered softly in his ear. "You wanted to be called early to do your practicing."

"Yes, Mama, I'll come right away," replied Harry, climbing out of bed. "I want to get in an hour of practice before breakfast."

Harry was taking lessons on the piano. First, his mother had started to teach him, but now he was taking lessons from a regular piano teacher in Kansas City. He was eager to learn and got up early every morning to practice so that neither work nor play would interfere.

Moments after Harry jumped out of bed, he

sat down before the piano and started to move his fingers deftly over the keys. First he had to practice scales and exercises, which he didn't particularly enjoy, but he knew that practicing them was necessary. "One-two-three-four, scales are boring," he said. "One-two-three-four, scales are boring."

Before long he changed the rhythm and muttered "One-two-three, time to waltz, one-two-three, time to waltz." He shifted smoothly from one rhythm to another, being careful to practice each of them well.

Near the end of the hour, he plunged gaily into the several musical selections which were included in his lesson. First he played a light selection from Mozart, and next a somewhat more difficult selection from Bach. Playing these selections seemed to take all the drudgery out of his preliminary practice.

After his hour of practice, Harry joined the

rest of the family for breakfast. "You're learning to play well," said his father. "We have enjoyed listening to you practice."

"Oh, good!" cried Harry. "I was afraid that you might get tired of hearing me practice scales and exercises. I love to play real pieces of music, but have to spend part of my time practicing other things, too."

"Of course," said his mother. "Don't worry about us becoming bored. We like to listen and are glad you are learning so rapidly."

"I've already done some of your chores this morning," interrupted Vivian. "I milked the cows while you were practicing."

"Oh, thank you," said Harry. "Now we can get an early start driving them to pasture. It will be fun to take them before people begin to use the streets."

The Trumans kept three cows which Harry and Vivian milked every morning and evening.

After they finished milking the cows in the morning, they drove them to a pasture about a mile out in the country. In the evening they brought them back from the pasture to the barn. Then they milked them again and left them in the barn or the fenced-in yard all night.

Harry and Vivian dashed from the house bareheaded and barefooted. They opened a gate and let the cows out into the street. "I'll bet they wonder why we're taking them so early this morning," said Vivian. "They'll surely have a good long day for eating grass."

"Yes, but that will be good," said Harry. "The more grass they eat today, the more milk they will give."

As the boys expected, they found very few people on the street so early in the morning. One was a friend of their father, who was just leaving his home to go to work. "You boys seem to be taking the cows to pasture extra early this morning," he called. "Why do you happen to be taking them so early?"

Vivian called back, "Harry got up at five o'clock this morning to practice his piano lesson, and while he was practicing I surprised him by milking the cows."

"Yes, Vivian surprised me this morning," said Harry. "Usually we don't milk the cows until after breakfast, so it is much later when we take them to pasture."

"You boys certainly are great helpers around home," said the man. "Your father has told me how hard you work and how trustworthy you are. He says that you are better than a couple of hired hands."

"Thank you, sir," said Harry. "We especially like to work with animals. Besides these cows, we take care of my father's horses, our two goats, and my black Shetland pony. We always look after them before we do anything else."

"That's fine," said the man. "If you keep on, you'll make a couple of good Missouri farmers when you grow up."

The boys followed the cows slowly along the streets and finally along the road to the pasture. "Cows surely walk slowly," said Harry. "I wish there was some way to make them walk faster so we could save time."

"Well, we might hit them with switches or throw rocks at them, but we wouldn't want to hurt them," said Vivian doubtfully.

"Oh, no," said Harry. "I don't want to hurt any animal. That's why I never go hunting with anybody. I just can't get any fun out of shooting at anything that can't shoot back."

At last the boys reached the pasture with the three cows. Vivian opened the big swinging gate to let them enter. Slowly they ambled away and started to nibble the green grass.

"Let's pace ourselves on the way back

home," suggested Harry. "Then we'll get there much faster than if we just saunter along."

"Pace ourselves?" questioned Vivian. "What do you mean?"

"We can count to help us walk at a steady pace," explained Harry. "We'll need to count in thousands, as one thousand one, one thousand two, one thousand three, one thousand four, and so on. Then we should be able to take two steps every time we say a number."

"Let's try," said Vivian. "That sounds as if it would be fun."

At once the boys started to count and walk briskly along the road toward home. They kept up a steady pace and were surprised by how quickly they arrived. By pacing himself in this manner, Harry developed a fondness for fast walking. Later in life he became noted for his habit of taking brisk morning walks.

When the boys reached home, they went to

the barn to take care of the black Shetland pony and their father's horses, all of which needed to be fed and watered. Harry put feed in their mangers, and Vivian pumped water to fill a big watering trough near the barn.

While the horses and pony were still eating, the boys started to curry them. Each boy curried an animal by himself. "I think I'll start with my pony," said Harry.

"First I'll do Papa's big gray horse," said Vivian. "He said something about wanting to ride him this afternoon."

"It's strange that we can't work together currying an animal, with one of us currying one side and the other currying the other side," commented Harry, "but, boy, that won't work. Do you remember the time when we tried to curry the same horse?"

"Yes, and I remember how the horse acted," said Vivian. "He shook his head and snorted,

138

slammed us against the sides of the stall, and tried to get rid of us."

Without further conversation, the two boys started to work, Harry on his pony and Vivian on the big gray horse. Skillfully they curried the animals to remove stray particles from their hair and then brushed them to make their hair look smooth and shiny. Both animals seemed to enjoy the currying and the brushing.

Later the boys turned the horses and pony loose in the fenced-in back yard or small field. Then they walked about to inspect their goats and a few partly grown calves which were running loose in the yard. "They seem to be all right this morning," said Harry.

Just as the boys started to return to the barn from inspecting the goats and calves, they noticed their father repairing a nearby fence. "We have just finished our chores and can help you if you need us," said Harry.

"No, I don't need any help here," replied Mr. Truman, "but I just noticed that the weeds have almost taken over the garden. Suppose you spend the rest of the forenoon hoeing and weeding the garden."

This job of hoeing and weeding the garden was tedious work which had to be done over and over again. The ground had to be loosened by chopping it with hoes and the weeds had to be chopped out or pulled out. Everything had to be done carefully in order not to damage the vegetables which were growing.

Without a word of objection, the boys walked off toward the garden. "If you finish the garden this forenoon, you may take the afternoon off for playing," called their father. "I am sure that some of your Waldo Avenue friends will turn up to join you."

"I know, but work comes first," said Harry. "If we don't finish the garden this forenoon, we can readily put off playing. After all, we can play any time."

The boys worked hard in the garden the rest of the forenoon, but still had part of it left to do. That afternoon when their friends came to play, Harry politely told them to come back some other time. Just now he and Vivian had more important things to do.

Thus work always came first with the two Truman boys. They had to work in order to earn a chance to play, but they didn't mind.

People
More Important

ONE MORNING the steady sound of *crack, chop, crack, chop* rang through the Truman back yard. Harry and Vivian were busy splitting chunks of wood into sticks for stovewood. The chunks had recently been delivered from a nearby woods.

Harry worked on one side of the wood pile and Vivian on the other. Each boy upended a chunk of wood and swung an ax to make a split place in one end. Then he put the blade of an iron wedge in the split place and tapped it a couple of times with the blunt side of the ax. Finally he gave the wedge a solid blow with

142

the blunt side of the ax to split the chunk into halves. If the chunk failed to split, he gave the wedge a solid blow again.

In a similar manner the boys split each half chunk into smaller and smaller pieces until the pieces were slender enough to put into the kitchen stove. Usually they had to split each chunk into eight or ten pieces to get them small enough to use.

In a short while the boys' father stopped at the wood pile on his way to the barn. He noticed how hard they were working and said, "You are doing a fine job. Already you have a good pile of sticks ready for the kitchen."

"It takes lots of wood to keep us going," said Harry. "Every day or so we have to come out here and split some more chunks."

"Yes, but we're lucky to live in a country where we have plenty of wood," said his father. "I don't know what we would do without it."

"I know," said Harry. "At school I enjoy reading how the early settlers cut down trees to get wood when they first came to America. They not only used wood for fuel, but they built cabins out of wood. They made furniture and many tools out of wood."

"That's right," said his father. "The early settlers were fortunate to find much of the land here covered with trees. If it hadn't been for all this wooded land, America never could have prospered as it has. Trees helped the people to get started."

"We still use wood almost as much as the settlers did," said Harry. "We use wood for heating and cooking. Our house and barn are made of wood. Our furniture is made of wood. Our wagon and buggy are made mostly of wood and even this ax has a wooden handle."

"One of our greatest uses of wood is to help keep the kitchen going," said his father. "Right now Aunt Caroline probably is using some of the wood which you have split here to make a fresh batch of bread. Later, when you stop to rest for a while, she may let you have a piece or two to eat."

Aunt Caroline was a pleasant Negro woman who helped their mother and grandmother with the cooking. She liked both boys and gave them loving attention along with good food. At the same time she was very strict with them, especially about keeping the wood box filled.

After the boys' father left, they kept thinking about the fresh bread which Aunt Caroline was baking. Soon they decided to go to the house to investigate. First, Vivian filled his arms with freshly split sticks of wood to put into the wood box. Seconds later, Harry followed with another armful.

"My goodness," cried Aunt Caroline. "You boys must be tuckered out from splitting all that wood. Would you like a little something to bolster your strength before you go back to the woodpile again?"

"We surely would," answered Harry. "What do you have to bolster the strength of a couple of tired workers?"

"Well, I have a fresh batch of bread which I have just taken from the oven," said Aunt Caroline, "and Mary Jane has just finished churning a fresh batch of butter. If you ask her politely, she might cut off a slice of hot bread for each of you and spread it with some of her fresh yellow butter."

Mary Jane grinned as she laid down a little wooden paddle with which she had been stirring the fresh butter in a wooden bowl. After she had finished churning, she had dipped out the chunks of butter and put them in this wooden bowl. Now she had just worked the butter into one large roll ready for use.

"How about it, Mary Jane?" begged Vivian. "Will you please spread us a couple of slices of bread with some of your fresh butter before you put it in the cellar to cool?"

"Yes," said Harry, "we're asking you politely just as Aunt Caroline suggested. Will you please spread us a couple of slices of bread with your fresh butter?"

"Of course for a couple of hard workers like you, I will," replied Mary Jane.

She quickly spread two pieces of fresh bread and Aunt Caroline poured out two glasses of milk. The boys went outside and sat on the back steps to eat. "Thank both of you," Harry called back. "We're surely lucky to have such good cooks in the kitchen."

After the boys finished eating, they went back to splitting wood. By now it was threatening to rain and they wanted to get as much wood split before noon as possible.

About an hour later their friend, Jim Wright, whistled to them, opened the gate, and strode over to them. "Hello, Harry and Viv," he called. "You boys seem to have your work cut out for you this morning."

"We surely have," answered Harry. "Splitting one chunk will entitle you to one bite of fresh bread, and splitting two chunks will entitle you to two bites. What do you say?"

"No, thank you," replied Jim. Then, turning to Vivian, he said, "I hear you have a new pair of fantailed pigeons in the barn. Can you stop long enough to show them to me?"

"I'm afraid not," said Vivian, "because we want to finish this job if we can. Why don't you come back right after lunch while we're resting for a while? Then I'll be glad to show you the pigeons."

"Yes, come back after lunch," said Harry. "While you're here looking at Viv's pigeons, I'll

148

read a book about people. After all, people are more important than pigeons."

That afternoon Jim returned and Vivian took him directly to the barn to see the new pigeons. Harry went to his room, picked up a book about the lives of presidents, and went to the barn, too. Quietly he climbed to the hayloft

and looked for a comfortable place to stretch out on the soft bed of hay. Moments later he opened the book to a section about Thomas Jefferson and started to read as follows:

"Jefferson, Thomas (1743–1826), was the third President of the United States and the principal author of the Declaration of Independence. Later in life he prepared his own epitaph to be placed on his grave. This epitaph, which reads as follows, indicates his pride in three achievements: 'Here lies buried Thomas Jefferson, author of the Declaration of Independence, The Statute of Virginia for Religious Freedom, and Father of the University of Virginia.'"

Just as Harry finished reading this paragraph about Jefferson, he heard raindrops beginning to fall on the roof of the barn. The sound of the steady patter of raindrops on the roof and the continuous voices of Jim and Vivian talking about pigeons in another part of the barn lulled him into a state of drowsiness. As he tried to read on, his thoughts became confused between napping and reading. "Jefferson—noted for Louisiana Purchase—pretty fantail pigeons —Jefferson served two terms as President—I hope to get some fantail pigeons—it's important to know how great men have solved important problems—raise fantail pigeons to sell —sometime I may need to know much about great men—I must keep awake."

Harry Truman did not merely repeat shallow words in reading but looked for important ideas. He read this book about the lives of Presidents and many other historical books from cover to cover.

Yes, for Harry people were more important than pigeons, not only during a rainy afternoon but during every day of his life.

Active Teenager

"YES, SIR, Mr. Clinton," said Harry one evening in September. "I will be here promptly at six-thirty Monday morning. Thank you for giving me this opportunity to work for you."

Harry, now fourteen years old, took rapid strides homeward. He actually was shorter than most boys of his age, but tonight he felt very tall inside. He just had obtained his first real job away from home.

When he stepped inside the house, he proudly shouted to the members of his family, "Get ready to listen to an important announcement. I have some big news for you."

"What do you mean by big news?" asked Vivian. "Come on and tell us about it."

"I have a job at Clinton's Drugstore," said Harry, "working each morning before I go to school and all day Saturday."

"That's wonderful," cried Mary Jane, "but how will you get in so early in the morning?"

"Mr. Clinton has given me a key to the front door," replied Harry. He pulled a big key from his pocket and placed it on the table where everybody could see it.

"Oh, my!" sighed Mama. "I'm afraid for you to carry that important key. You must be very careful not to lose it."

"Don't worry, Mama," said Harry. "I'll be sure to hang on to it."

"What work will you do at the store before it opens in the morning?" asked Vivian.

"First I'll scrub and rinse the floor, sweep the sidewalk, and dust the counters," replied

Harry. "Then I'll do odd jobs until I have to leave for school. Monday morning, for instance, I'll begin to dust shelves and wipe off bottles. It probably will take me several days to do all the shelves and bottles in the store."

"That surely sounds like an easy job to me," teased Vivian. "I wish I could get an easy job to earn some extra money."

"Well, you may think that it sounds easy, but Mr. Clinton warned me that it will be just the opposite. He says that keeping a store clean and orderly is hard work."

On Monday morning, slightly before six-thirty, Harry proudly turned the key in the front door of Clinton's Drugstore. Immediately he got out two big buckets and two big mops for scrubbing and rinsing the floor. He filled one bucket with soapy water for scrubbing and the other with clean water for rinsing.

Moments later he dipped the big scrub mop

into the bucket of soapy water and started to push it over the floor. "My, this mop filled with water seems heavier than a pitchfork loaded with hay," he thought. "Why do people think that mopping is easier than pitching hay?"

Harry worked steadily until he finished scrubbing and rinsing the floor. He looked all around to make sure that every part of the floor was clean and shining. Then he put the scrub buckets and mops away.

Next he got out two push brooms, or brushes, for cleaning in front of the store. One broom was for cleaning the sidewalk and the other, which was slightly wider, was for cleaning the gutter. "I've helped Mama sweep many times at home," he thought, "but pushing these brooms will be entirely different."

He started at one corner of the building and pushed the narrower broom along the sidewalk entirely across the front. Then he turned and pushed it away from the building to dump the dust and litter into the gutter. Back and forth he went in this manner until he finished sweeping the entire sidewalk. Next he swept the gutter with the wider broom and put the dirt and litter in a big metal container. Finally he inspected both the sidewalk and gutter to make sure they were clean.

As he turned to go back inside, he noticed Mr. Clinton coming along the sidewalk toward the drugstore. "Good morning there, Harry," he called cheerfully. "How are you getting along with your work this morning?"

At first Harry was too surprised to answer, but at last he managed to say, "All right, I believe, only I haven't finished yet. Is it time for me to go to school?"

"No, don't worry," said Mr. Clinton. "I just came a little early this morning to see whether you might need any help."

"Well, I have finished mopping and rinsing the floor and sweeping the sidewalk and gutter," explained Harry. "Now I'm ready to go inside to dust the counters."

The two of them stepped inside the drugstore and Mr. Clinton looked down at the shiny clean floor. "You have done a wonderful job on both the floor and sidewalk," he said.

Harry finished dusting the counters and still had a little time left before he needed to leave for school. Mr. Clinton took him to a corner of the store to explain how to dust the shelves and wipe off the bottles of medicine. "You'll have to be careful in handling the bottles," he said, "because they'll break easily."

As Harry started to wipe the bottles, he noticed that many of them had peculiar labels. He asked Mr. Clinton about them and learned that they were Latin abbreviations. Then he wondered whether the Latin which he was studying in high school would help him to read any of the abbreviations on the bottles.

All week, morning after morning, Harry went to the store regularly to carry on his duties. Saturday evening after he had finished his work for the day, Mr. Clinton handed him three silver dollars. "Here is your first week's salary, Harry," he said. "You are off to a good start working for me."

From the drugstore Harry hurried straight home. He burst into the house, still carrying the three silver dollars in his hand. "Here, Papa," he cried. "I have brought you three dollars to help you with your expenses."

"No, Harry, that money is yours," replied Mr. Truman. "I wouldn't think of taking any of it for family purposes."

Harry was both disappointed and happy. He had truly wanted to help his father, but he was glad still to have the money. Later, when he went to bed, he placed the three dollars close by where he could reach out and touch them in case he awakened during the night.

Harry worked at the drugstore only a few months. Soon his parents suggested that he quit working so he would have more time for study. "You always have been a fine student," they said. "We don't want anything to interfere with your getting a good education."

Harry fully realized that this was a sensible suggestion and promptly resigned his job. "I want to get good grades," he said, "because I soon must begin to think about the future."

Frequently after he quit working at the drugstore, he went over to his Aunt Ella's house to study. His Aunt Ella was his mother's sister, who had two daughters in high school, Cousins Nellie and Ethel. "By studying together, we can help one another," they said.

Other boys and girls came to Aunt Ella's

home to study with Nellie and Ethel. One was Bess Wallace, who now was Harry's classmate. Usually they gathered around a big dining room table, where they could spread out their books and tablets.

Besides studying hard in high school, Harry took part in a variety of activities. When he was a senior, he helped one of his friends, Charles Ross, to start a new high school paper, called *The Gleam*. Years later, when Truman became President, he selected Charles Ross to serve as his press secretary.

Through these years Harry maintained a strong interest in politics. In 1900 he had an opportunity to serve as page at the Democratic National Convention, which was held in Kansas City. He shouted with glee as he watched and heard the delegates nominate William Jennings Bryan to be the candidate for President.

As Harry approached the end of his high

school years, he became more and more concerned about the future. Always he had hoped to attend college through partial help from his parents, but during his last year in high school his father suddenly lost most of his property.

Harry now investigated the possibility of obtaining an appointment to the United States Military Academy at West Point, New York, or the United States Naval Academy at Annapolis, Maryland. He actually started to study for taking the entrance examinations at one or both these institutions, but his hopes were short-lived. He was rejected in a physical examination because of the condition of his eyes.

Thus, in 1901, seventeen-year-old Harry S. Truman graduated from Independence High School with no specific plans for the future. He had faith, however, that in our democratic way of life he would find a way.

From Farm to President

Young Harry S. Truman possessed stamina or the will to carry on despite disappointments. Even though he had no definite plans for the future when he graduated from high school, he possessed determination and the willingness to work. Not for one moment did he harbor the idea that the world owed him a living.

During the first few years after he graduated, he held several jobs. First, he became timekeeper for a gang of construction workers on the Sante Fe Railroad. Next he worked briefly wrapping newspapers in the mailing room of the *Kansas City Star*. Finally he became a bookkeeper, first at the National Bank of Commerce, and later at the Union National Bank, in Kansas City. Often on Saturdays he worked as an usher at the Grand Theater in Kansas City. Also during these years he joined the Missouri National Guard and attended practice sessions regularly.

After both Harry and Vivian graduated from high school, their parents moved back to live with Grandma Young on the big farm near Grandview. Once more John Truman took over the job of managing the farm. In the meantime Harry and Vivian lived at a boarding house in Kansas City.

In 1906 John Truman offered to turn over the management of the farm to Harry. He knew that even though Harry was starting a business career, he still was deeply interested in farming. At once Harry left his position in the bank in Kansas City to take over the management of the farm. There he started a successful career that lasted more than ten years.

During these years young Truman did nearly every kind of work possible on a farm. On the side, however, he found time to take part in local politics and to help found a county farm bureau organization. Gradually he came to be regarded as a forceful community leader.

Young Truman's farm experiences were marred by two great personal losses from death. In 1909 Grandma Young, whom he had affectionately loved since early childhood, passed away. In 1915 his father, John Truman, whom he had always trusted for parental guidance, died suddenly following an accident.

All the time that young Truman ran the farm he made frequent trips to Kansas City and Independence to visit old friends. Chief among his friends was Bess Wallace, whom he began to visit regularly. Finally he purchased a sec-

ond-hand automobile which he kept neatly pol-
ished and used chiefly for going to see her.

Young Truman's first real opportunity to
serve his country came in the spring of 1917,
when the United States entered World War I.
As a member of the Missouri National Guard,
he helped to organize a regiment in the field
artillery. Shortly after he started training, he
was commissioned a Lieutenant.

Early in 1918 he was sent to France, where
he was promoted to Captain. From then on, he
engaged in the thick of the conflict until No-
vember 11, 1918, when an Armistice, or cease-
fire, went into effect. Following the Armistice,
he stayed on in Europe for several months to
carry on post-war duties. In May, 1919, he was
discharged with the rank of Major.

Back in Independence, Bess Wallace had
been waiting patiently for her future husband
to return. About eight weeks later, they were

married in the Trinity Episcopal Church in Independence. After a short wedding trip, they settled down in a big frame house at 219 North Delaware Street in Independence. This lovely old house, which had been built by Bess's grandfather, served as the Truman home from then on except for his years in Washington.

Soon after the war, Truman helped to start a haberdashery in Kansas City. He worked hard to make the business a success, but unfortunately it failed. Subsequently he turned to politics and was elected district judge in Jackson County, Missouri. In this position, he helped to manage the business affairs of the county. He was not a judge in a court of law.

As district judge, young Harry S. Truman proved to be very efficient and popular. In 1926 he was elected Presiding Judge of Jackson County, and four years later was overwhelmingly reelected to the same office. During these eight years he was the chief managing officer of Jackson County. In 1934 he was nominated as the Democratic candidate for the United States Senate from Missouri. He easily won the election and now was ready to move into a much larger sphere of political activities.

Senator Harry S. Truman, his wife Bess, and their daughter Margaret, now ten years old, promptly moved to Washington, D.C. In his first term as Senator, he gained a notable reputation for his studious nature and dependability in office. In 1940 he was elected to his second term as United States Senator.

After World War II started in Europe in 1939, the United States government began a huge military preparedness program, lest we be drawn into the conflict. It spent huge sums of money to procure military equipment and supplies, such as airplanes, warships, and munitions, and to modernize military training centers. Shortly after these efforts began, Senator Truman became suspicious that much money was being wasted. He made a careful study of military expenditures for supplies and discovered many contracts in which both business and labor were profiteering at government expense.

Finally, in 1941, about the time the United States actively entered the war, Senator Truman was appointed chairman of a special Senate committee to investigate the national defense program. This committee discovered many cases of careless spending and saved the country huge sums of money. Mr. Truman, as chairman, attained great publicity and the committee came to be known as the Truman Committee.

Through these years President Franklin D. Roosevelt came to have very high regard for Senator Truman and his committee's activities. In 1944, when he was nominated by the National Democratic Convention for his fourth term as President, he chose Harry S. Truman to be his running mate for Vice-President. In the fall election they won an overwhelming victory. On January 20, 1945, Mr. Roosevelt was inaugurated for his fourth term as President, and Mr. Truman was inaugurated as Vice-President.

During the succeeding weeks President Roosevelt was so busily engaged directing war activities that he had very little time to confer with Vice-President Truman. Furthermore he was beginning to suffer ill health from the long strain of heavy responsibilities in office. Finally, in April, 1945, he went to Warm Springs, Georgia, for a much-needed rest.

On April 12, less than three months after Mr. Truman had become Vice-President, he received an urgent call from President Roosevelt's wife, Eleanor, to come to the White House. When he arrived, she informed him

that the President had just died in Warm Springs and that he would have to take over the duties as President.

This message was a great shock to Mr. Truman. He felt sorry for Mrs. Roosevelt and asked what he could do for her. In reply she asked what she could do for him. "In assuming the tremendous burdens of President," she said, "you are the one who will need help."

Immediately special arrangements were made for a swearing-in ceremony in the Cabinet Room at the White House. There, in the presence of his wife Bess, his daughter Margaret, members of the cabinet, and other top government officials, Harry S. Truman took the oath to become our thirty-third President.

From the beginning the people had great confidence in Mr. Truman as President. Already he had won high esteem for his many evidences of good judgment and integrity in office.

The Buck Stops Here

PRESIDENT Harry S. Truman accepted the responsibilities of his high office with great humility. The United States still was involved in World War II, both in Europe and in the Pacific. Fortunately, the Allied forces were fast winning in Germany and it was apparent that the war in Europe would soon end. On the other hand the war in the Pacific was still bitter and might go on for some time.

From the beginning, President Truman realized that he must continue the foreign policies which President Roosevelt had inaugurated. He must maintain close relations with our allies, which included some of the leading nations of the world. He must find out what agreements had been made with them and what agreements still needed to be made.

A few months prior to Roosevelt's death, our allies and other free nations of the world had arranged to hold an important conference on April 25, 1945, in San Francisco, California. The purpose of the meeting was to set up a world organization to maintain peace in the world following the war. President Truman officially greeted all the delegates in Washington, D.C., before they met in San Francisco.

On May 8, 1945, less than two weeks after this important meeting started in San Francisco, the war in Europe came to an end. Germany surrendered and the victorious Allies proclaimed Victory in Europe Day, commonly known as V-E Day, to the world. President Truman immediately went on radio to relay the glad news to the American people. While speaking, however, he emphasized the fact that our victory was only half won, that we still had to defeat Japan in the Pacific. In conclusion, he called for united support in continuing the struggle.

For weeks, the delegates from the free nations continued their negotiations in San Francisco. During this period they received helpful guidance from President Truman and other world leaders. Finally they worked out an agreement, or charter, for establishing a world-wide peace organization to be known as the United Nations.

On June 26, 1945, President Truman flew to San Francisco to address the delegates and to witness the signing of the new United Nations Charter. Later the United States Senate ratified the Charter, enabling us to cooperate with other nations in working for peace.

In July, 1945, President Truman flew to Potsdam, Germany, to meet with Prime Minister Winston Churchill of Great Britain and Premier Joseph Stalin of the Soviet Union. The purpose of this meeting was to discuss means of restoring peaceful conditions to Europe and means of intensifying the war against Japan. From Potsdam they urged Japan to surrender or face the possibility of destruction.

For several years the United States had been working secretly on a powerful new weapon called the atomic bomb. This bomb was so powerful that it could destroy a whole city in a single explosion. As the war with Japan dragged on with no indications of surrender, President Truman began to consider the possibility of using this bomb. He was eager to halt the tremendous sacrifice of life which was occurring each day. Finally he approved dropping the atomic bomb on a Japanese city.

On August 5, 1945, an airplane dropped an atomic bomb on Hiroshima, which laid the city in ruins. Japan still ignored peace proposals, and four days later another airplane dropped an atomic bomb on Nagasaki, which laid that city in ruins. Immediately thereafter Japan agreed to surrender. Thus President Truman's bold action terminated a war that might have dragged on for years.

The official Japanese surrender, known as V-J Day, took place on September 2, 1945, aboard the *U.S.S. Missouri* in Tokyo Bay. This ship, which had been named after President Truman's home state, was a very appropriate location for the meeting. His daughter, Margaret, had christened the ship and he himself had spoken during the christening ceremony.

The American people happily celebrated the end of the war. To many it meant that sons, husbands, brothers, and fathers soon would be coming home. It meant that they no longer needed to live in fear that their loved ones would be killed or lost.

After the celebration was over, the country faced the problem of bringing huge numbers of servicemen home. Some clamored for the men to be brought home immediately. Others felt that they should be brought back gradually so they could find jobs and settle down at work. President Truman resolved this problem by asking Congress to pass the Servicemen's Readjustment Act, commonly known as the G. I. Bill of Rights. This bill provided a year's pay for unemployed veterans, which slowed down their search for jobs after they returned.

Another important problem after the war was the readjustment of prices and wages. During the war, prices and wages had been rigidly controlled. At once, both business and labor wanted the controls lifted. Companies wanted to charge higher prices for their products, and labor wanted to obtain higher wages. When the government lifted the controls, President Truman urged both business and labor to exercise rigid controls of their own. At one time he even considered asking Congress to pass a law which would draft workers into the armed services if they made unreasonable demands for increases in wages.

While Truman was handling these problems at home, he faced many serious problems abroad. Soon after the war, it became apparent that the Soviet Union was determined to promote the spread of Communism in the world. One of its plans was to take over weak countries bordering the Mediterranean Sea, including Greece and Turkey.

Promptly President Truman came forth with a bold plan to save these countries from being taken over by the Soviet Union. He asked Congress to grant both countries financial aid to strengthen their governments and living conditions. This policy of granting financial aid to countries threatened with communist aggression became known as the Truman Doctrine.

Next it became apparent that the Soviet Union was planning to take over certain countries in Western Europe, all of which were having financial troubles following the war. President Truman, with the help of George C. Marshall, Secretary of State, worked out a system of granting financial aid to countries which were willing to help themselves. This system, which came to be known as the Marshall Plan, proved to be a tremendous force in helping countries to combat the spread of communism.

About this time, the Soviet Union attempted to blockade the highway leading from West Germany to the city of Berlin, which now was a part of West Germany but was completely surrounded by the communist country of East Germany. Under the terms of the treaty following the war, this highway was supposed to be left open to traffic between Berlin and West Germany. In a bold maneuver Truman joined with England in arranging for airplanes to carry food, fuel, medicines, and other necessary products into Berlin. Several months later the Soviet Union gave up the blockade and allowed the highway to be opened.

Early in 1948 the new United Nations, with encouragement from President Truman, passed a resolution recommending the formation of a new country for Jews in the Holy Land of western Asia. For centuries the Jews had had no country of their own but had lived in scattered countries of the world. Soon the Jews founded the new country of Israel and the United States was the first country in the world to recognize it as a sovereign state.

In 1948 the Democratic National Convention proudly nominated Truman for election to a full term as President, and the Republican National Convention nominated Thomas E. Dewey, Governor of New York, as the opposing candidate. President Truman put on an extensive speaking campaign. He drew large enthusiastic crowds, but many newspapers and public opinion polls predicted his defeat.

On election night the first returns showed Dewey running ahead, but when all the votes were tabulated, President Truman was re-elected. One large newspaper was so sure that Dewey would win that it printed and started to sell an edition carrying the headline, "Dewey Defeats Truman." The President considered this error a great joke and even had his photograph taken with a copy of the newspaper.

Following the election, President Truman strenuously continued his efforts to promote peace in the world. In the spring of 1949 the representatives of ten countries of Europe and of the United States and Canada met in Washington, D. C., to sign a treaty forming the North Atlantic Treaty Organization, commonly called NATO. This organization has served as a powerful force for peace.

In 1950 problems over the spread of Communism erupted in Asia. North Korea, which was a Communist country backed by the Soviet Union, invaded the Republic of Korea, its neighbor to the south. President Truman, with the support of Congress, decided to send troops to help protect South Korea. Later, the United Nations approved Truman's actions, and several other countries sent troops to help protect South Korea. General Douglas MacArthur, who had won distinction in fighting against Japan in World War II, was chosen to command the United Nations troops.

At first, the United Nations' troops under General MacArthur pushed the North Korean forces back, but a huge army from Communist China invaded South Korea to assist the North Korean forces. General MacArthur wanted to invade Communist China, but President Truman objected to extending the military operations to other countries. In return, General MacArthur publicly disagreed with President Truman's policy. Finally the President dismissed General MacArthur from service, and the war dragged on during the remainder of his administration.

All the while Mr. Truman was engaged in foreign relations, he handled many domestic problems. On one occasion he prevented a serious railroad strike by sending soldiers to operate the railroads. On another occasion he prevented a serious steel mill strike by sending soldiers to take over the mills. He handled all domestic problems courageously, regardless of public opinion, favorable or unfavorable.

During his second term, he encouraged the Congress to propose an amendment to the United States Constitution to limit the tenure of a President to two four-year terms by election of the people. This amendment, which was ratified by a majority of the states, exempted Truman from its provisions because he hadn't been elected to two full terms by the people. There was much clamor for him to run again, but he promptly declined.

During the time he was President, he witnessed many advances in the means of communication. On October 5, 1947, when he delivered his first television address from the White House, he was the first President ever to appear on television. The coming of television helped to bring the office of the Presidency of our country much closer to the people.

186

When Truman left the Presidency on January 20, 1953, he and Mrs. Truman and their daughter Margaret moved back to their home at 219 North Delaware Street, Independence, Missouri. About three years later Margaret married Elbert Clifton Daniel, Jr., a prominent journalist with the *New York Times*. From this time on, she made her home in New York.

Soon after Truman retired to Independence, he began to write his memoirs, or a history of his experiences in the White House. His first book, *Volume I: Year of Decisions,* was published in 1955, and his second book, *Volume II: Years of Trial and Hope,* was published in 1956. Both books were eagerly and widely read by the American people.

While Mr. Truman was writing these memoirs, his friends and associates erected a huge building in Independence, known as the Truman Library, to honor him. This building included an office which he could use as his personal headquarters and space for storing and preserving all the personal records and mementos which he had accumulated as President. He began to occupy his office in 1957.

Here he continued to read, write, and carry on his extensive correspondence. Here he entertained his former governmental associates and other important persons, when they came to visit him. Here he met groups of school children who came to the library.

Of all Mr. Truman's visitors, his favorites were his four grandsons. His daughter Margaret and her husband had four sons, named Clifton Truman, William Wallace, Harrison Gates, and Thomas Washington. All were close pals of their distinguished grandfather.

One of the most interesting exhibits at the Library is a replica of Mr. Truman's presidential office in the White House. The chair is the actual chair in which he sat as President, but all the other furnishings are duplicated. When a President finishes his term in Washington, all he can take from his office is his chair.

On top of the replica of President Truman's desk is a desk piece with a motto which reads, "The Buck Stops Here." While he was President he wanted people to know that he assumed responsibility for everything he did.

The motto on the other side of the desk piece reads, "I'm from Missouri." This motto refers to an old familiar Missouri expression, "I'm from Missouri, show me." Mr. Truman always welcomed suggestions, but he wanted proof that they were honest and sincere.

At first Mr. Truman wanted the Truman Library to be built on the big farm near Grandview, where he had spent many years of his life. By now, however, a large shopping center has been built on this farm and named in honor of the Truman family. A tablet at the center contains the following tribute:

"Two boys, Harry S. Truman and J. Vivian Truman, and their sister, Mary Jane Truman, once lived on, worked, and ploughed the farmland on which this shopping center now stands. In the great American tradition, one boy went from these fields to become President of the United States. The brother and sister became outstanding civic leaders.

Now, in one lifetime, the farm again contributes to the great American dream of opportunity and progress by becoming the site of one of the nation's finest shopping centers—Truman Corners Town and Country Shoppers' City—dedicated to the Truman family, the people of Greater Kansas City, and all the United States—This could happen only in America."

In Lamar, Missouri, the house where Harry S. Truman was born has been preserved as the President Truman Birthplace Memorial Shrine.

A large limestone monument has been built in front of the house. The following record has been carved on one side of the monument:

County Judge, 1923–25
Presiding Judge County Court, 1927–1935
United States Senator, 1935–1945
Vice-President of the United States of America, 1945
President of the United States of America, 1945–1953

Through the years many important events were held in nearby Kansas City to honor Mr. Truman. One was a huge birthday party which was held on or near May 8 of each year at the Muehlebach Hotel in Kansas City. Friends from all parts of the country came to attend this famous party.

While Mr. Truman was speaking at the party which was held on his eightieth birthday, he expressed a hope to live at least ten more years. He recalled that his mother had lived to be ninety-four years old, and that her father had lived to be ninety-one. Thus longevity seemed to run in the family.

From this time on, despite Mr. Truman's hope, his health gradually failed and he suffered several serious illnesses. Each year he seemed to grow weaker and finally he had to give up taking the early morning walks for which he had become noted. He died December 26, 1972, in a Kansas City hospital at the age of eighty-eight.

Harry S. Truman was buried in a rose garden near the Truman Library in Independence. This library serves as a fitting memorial to a Missouri farm boy who rose to the high office of President. He served with distinction during some of the most trying years in history.